CONTENTS

I	A TURN OF THE WHEEL	5
II	THE HANDS OF WAR	16
III	FIGHTING AMONG OURSELVES	24
IV	GOING AWAY AND STAYING AT HOME	30
V	FOOD ON THE TABLE	41
VI	RECEIVING	58
VII	FORBIDDEN FRUIT	66
VIII	A STRONG AND PERFECT CHRISTIAN	77
IX	THE REAPER COMES	85
X	THE STATIONS	92
XI	AT THE THRESHING	100
XII	BY TRAIN TO THE SEASIDE	107
XIII	THE LIGHT OF THE FIRE	118
XIV	CHRISTMAS	125
XV	THE APPRENTICE	140
XVI	FUGITIVE	155
XVII	STRAWBOYS COME DANCING	170
XVIII	GOODBYE TO THE HILLS	181

I

A TURN OF THE WHEEL

I was just six months old when I was brought to the house in Carrigeen where I spent my life until I was twenty-three. I often heard about the journey and often too have I tried to imagine what it was like that morning as we drove in Danny Maurice O'Connor's sidecar from Shinnagh Cross to Carrigeen. I was born in March 1914 so it was a September day. I always see my father and mother on one wing of the jaunting car and me sitting on my mother's lap, Danny Maurice on the other wing and conversing with my father in a loud voice over the noise of the horse's hooves and the grinding of the iron-shod wheels on the road. All our belongings were on that car. My mother's personal possessions were stored in the well, as the deep receptacle at the back of the sidecar was called. There was a bundle on the box seat in front, and under the seat the tools of my father's trade. He was a carpenter. Some more things, probably bedclothes, on the seat beside the driver, and on the flat surface over the well a box my dad had made with tableware and maybe a kettle and a few pots.

If I took any notice of the countryside as we drove along I would have seen the behind-the-times farmers still making hay which had become a little discoloured because of bad weather. At this time the stalks would be beginning to fade in the potato gardens and men would be busy drawing out turf from the inner bog and stacking it by the roadside to be carted home later. I like to think of it as a sunny day; a pet day coming to brighten up the countryside after a lot of rain.

Then I would have seen the mountains that ring, or half-ring, that great saucer of land from Castleisland to the County Bounds. Their names are the first five beads on my rosary — the MacGillicuddy Reeks, Mangerton, Stoompa, Crohane, and to the east and looking down on our sidecar, the Paps. The old people called this twin mountain An Dá Chích Dannan, the two breasts of the goddess Dana. Maybe I wasn't looking, my mouth on another breast that sustained me. A Rathmore man told me once that when people climbed the Paps each man took a stone and placed it on one of the two cairns at the top of twin peaks. In time these two cairns grew to be the nipples on the breasts of Dana. Further upland towards Boharbue you can see the mountain range in its entirety and you can make out what looks like the torso of Dana stretched out in the sun. One breast, they say, is something higher than the other, as if she were lying a little on her side. Up there Fionn MacCumhaill stood and, bending down, he washed his face in the waters of Doocorrig Lake.

In the shade of the Paps were born the poets Eoghan Ruadh Ó Súilleabháin and Aodhagán Ó Rathaille. Each day as the sun shone they saw those perfect shapes against the sky, and maybe the old gods who lived up there inspired them. At the foot of the Paps is the City, Cathair Chroibh Dhearg, a ruined fort. When it was in its glory it was walled and circular like Dun Aengus or Staigue Fort. I see Crobh Dearg as a high priest of the pagans and his hand was red from slaughtering animals — and for all we know maybe humans

— as a sacrifice on the high altar when Our Lord was a boy or even before Homer nodded.

Since Christian times the City has been associated with Gobnait, the Ballyvourney saint. The first of May was the Pattern Day, a day of pilgrimage. From early morning the way was black with people going up the rising, twisting road to the ruined circle. The lame, the blind and the halt sat or lay by the roadside. They carried placards on their breasts or exposed a mortified limb, crying aloud their ailments and calling on our charity. Often I did the rounds at the City, walking inside and outside the circle, praying and pausing at a station marked by a rock fallen from the once high wall. The prayers, as far as I remember, were the Creed, the Our Father, three Hail Marys and a Glory be to the Father. At one station I waited my turn to take the pointed stone and draw the sign of the cross, three, five or seven times on the rock. From the rubbing of one stone on the other over the centuries the cross is worn deep into the rock. In my young days the bush beside the holy well was festooned with *giobals*, pieces torn from the pilgrims' clothing. At the base of the shrub, buttons, old combs, hairpins and safety pins were placed by pilgrims making the old pagan gesture of leaving their troubles behind. People prayed to be cured of their afflictions and once I saw a pair of crutches by the holy well.

To complete the round, the last thing a pilgrim did was to drink from the well and give a penny to the poor woman who filled the mug for him. The well was said to have curative properties and bottles of water from it were brought home to treat humans and animals. Traders' stalls, often in tents, were set up around the circle where sweet cakes, buns, apples and lemonade were sold. As evening fell, young boys and girls drifted away from their elders and danced to the music of the fiddle in Duggans' field.

The Paps looked down on our sidecar as we journeyed west. These twin mountains would colour my youth. When they donned their cloudy nightcap the weather was about to change. When they looked distant the coming week would be fine and when they were clapped up to you it would rain tomorrow. When a man was making something clear in conversation and that something wasn't readily grasped he would protest that the point that he was making was as plain as the Paps. A priest, new to the parish, had a jumble sale and a young lady bought a crocheted cardigan. It was very open crocheting, a string of holes tied together. The priest asked the girl's mother how her daughter liked the cardigan, and the mother said, 'It is like a screen, Father. You could see the Paps through it!'

'Ah,' the priest answered, 'can't she wear a blouse underneath?'

Crossing the railway bridge this side of the Bower, we came to a crossroads where a ghost was said to appear. The ghost was known as the Spirit of Béalnadeega. She waylaid and attacked men late at night. She was able to pull a rider from his horse and blind him by squirting her breastmilk into his eyes. Some held she was the evil sister of the goddess Dana or a female demon of that far-off age. The parish priest was helpless in his efforts to get rid of her. A very holy man, a friar, read over the spot where she used to appear and the spirit was never seen again. He banished her from Ireland, people said, and her penance was to drain the Dead Sea with a silver spoon for all eternity.

After climbing the steep hill above Barraduv Bridge we came to the village itself and my father asked the driver in for a drink. My mother thought we should keep on going but the men said it wouldn't take a minute. The horse stood outside the pub, well accustomed to such an exercise. The bar was dark, with a low ceiling and only a small window to allow in the light. We were well known in that house. My grandfather, on his way from town, was a regular customer there. The pony that pulled his tub trap stopped at John Dan's of her own accord.

When Kate Connie, the publican's wife, had filled the two pints for the men she took my mother into the kitchen. It was only then that Kate spotted me, wrapped in my mother's black shoulder shawl. I was held up to the light. The back door was opened to let in the sun and I was admired. 'What age is he? Who's he like? He's a Cash, I'd say!' She put a silver piece into my little fist and poked my middle playfully, saying, 'Kutsie, kutsie, kutsie!' She boiled the kettle to make a cup of tea. My mother would rather that than any alcoholic beverage. 'Drink!' she used to say. 'If you were spilling it at my feet I wouldn't touch it.'

When the men had finished – and I'd venture to say that they had two pints a man, reminding each other that a bird never flew on one wing – we set out, leaving our goodbyes with Kate Connie. We boarded the sidecar and began the last leg of our journey. We passed by the church that later in life I would attend every Sunday, down on one knee beside my father at the men's side and listening to the word of God. Once every five years I would hear the missionaries thunder in that small church.

We were passing now through countryside that would become familiar to me as the years went on. Not only would I come to know the name of each townland but in time I would learn the names of fields or some prominent feature of the landscape and the story behind each name. When we drew up outside our new home we were in the middle of the half-circle of mountains to the south. Mangerton, Ceapach and Stoompa I would see every day and watch their changing faces. The house was almost new and had become vacant because the tenant had died of consumption. In the three rooms there was a circular black mark, the size of a saucer, on the boards, where the disinfecting candle had burned itself into the floor. The Murphys, our new neighbours, who knew we were coming, had a fire down and had brought a jug of milk and some vegetables to go with our first meal. The few sticks of furniture were old but in time my father made a new bed, a better table, a few chairs and a dresser. The bed I remember best because I slept in it with my parents. It had a high board all round, the inside was filled with straw and on top of this was an enormous feather tick. My mother, when dressing the bed, would flounce this up and down and when the sheet was spread she would place me on the bed and I would sink gradually into the feather tick, laughing up at her as she tickled me.

My father was busy every day. He used the new kitchen table as a bench, and before he turned his hand to building a workshop at the gable of the house he made a cradle for me. My mother had had the use of Mrs Cronin's old cradle when we were living at Shinnagh Cross. The cradle my father made was a much swankier affair, with a hood and two rockers. On a fine day he'd lift the cradle out to the corner of the house along with a chair for my mother. She sat under the shining sun doing her knitting, rocking the cradle with her foot and singing to me as she kept her eye on our new cow in case she strayed out on to the road. A cow uneasy in her new surroundings would try to get back to where she came from. But when she had her calf she settled down. Then my mother had two youngsters to look after. The calf didn't drink all the cow's milk. There was plenty for the house and my mother skimmed the pan where it was set and made butter by shaking the cream in the big teapot.

The girls from Murphys' next door came to mind me if my mother had to do some shopping, doing the messages as it was called. When I was older they often told me what I looked like as an infant. They said I had a fine head of flaxen curls.

In time my mother got hens and a cock. When I could sit up in the cradle I loved watching this proud bird as he strutted through the yard with measured pace, his red comb like a crown on his head. I clapped my pudgy hands as he flapped his wings and crowed. There were two out offices going with the house. One of these was now turned into a fowl house, the other was later to become a piggery. My father had built a cowshed with space for a stable when we got the pony.

We were now well established, with a workshop at the gable end of the house and customers were coming. As well as being a carpenter my father was a wheelwright. When I was well able to stand up my mother would put me in a tea-chest in the workshop. My father as he worked could keep an eye on me and she was free to do whatever she wanted. The hens made nests in the workshop and a hen when she laid an egg proclaimed to all creation her great achievement. As she clucked her way to the door a ring of shavings would become entangled in her leg. She would drag it with her to the yard, trying to shake it off as she went. I chuckled at this and my father, seeing me laugh, laughed to himself and went on running the plane on the straight edge of the board.

Neighbours who came with an order sat for a while and watched my father working. 'A trade is as good as an estate,' they'd sometimes say. 'And a man who knows his trade well can hold his head high in any community!' The skill of making a wheel was the admiration of many. The materials for it were bought in Lord Kenmare's sawmills, all the wood grown locally: elm for the stock or hub, elm too for the felloes or rim and oak for the spokes. The stock was turned on the mill lathe, the felloes were sawn and the spokes split with the grain for strength, like a hurley stick. There was a special wheel-stool made by the carpenter for wheelmaking. It held the stock firm between four stool pins while it was being mortised to receive the twelve spokes. Each mortise was bored with an auger and finished with a chisel.

A sharp tool is the craftsman's friend and my father prided himself on being able to put up a good edge. Tools had to be ground down to cut away the proud steel behind the cutting edge, and for this purpose there was a grindstone. It was a wheel of sandstone which my mother turned. She twisted the handle with her right hand and poured the water on the wheel with her left, while my father held the chisel firmly on the sandstone. She complained that it was tiresome doing two things at the same time so my father, always inventive, made a wooden trough underneath to hold water. The wheel, when spun, went through the water and it was better than the old way, for an even amount of water was always on the wheel. When the chisel was ground, the sharpening was completed on an oilstone. Fast back and forward movements and then the front of the chisel laid flat on the stone to remove the burr. My father would clean the edge between his thumb and first finger and look at it closely in the light. If he was satisfied, he took up the wooden mallet and sent the chisel singing through the wood.

The stock mortised, my father turned his hand to the spokes. Each spoke was given a face. This was a straight flat surface made with the plane while the spoke was held firmly in the vice. Then with a drawing knife he shaped the spoke, an oval in cross-section, and finished it with the spoke shave.

The chips and shavings from the wood, in this case oak and elm, gave rise to a compound of smells. My small nose twitched and I thought the speckled hen coming from her nest twitched her beak a little too. The stock was fixed firmly in the wheel stool and each of the twelve spokes was driven home with a heavy hammer.

There was a mark on the stock at each side where it had been held in the lathe. A hole was bored in the front mark and a long arm called a trammel was screwed into it. This arm could be spun around and used to mark the ends of the spokes, equidistant from the stock. Dowels were formed at the ends to go into the felloes. My father placed the appropriate template on a roughly sawn felloe and marked it off, sawed it to the length and with a hatchet cut off the surplus wood on the convex side and with a tool called an adze shaped the concave surface. Holes were bored in the felloes to receive the spoke dowels and each felloe had a smaller dowel to connect them together. When the wheel was rimmed my father rolled it around my tea chest and said, 'Wheel'. I was too young to get my tongue around the word. All I could say was 'Dada'. I said that and it pleased him.

My mother brought me in her arms and put me sitting on the grass by the river the day of the wheel shoeing. The diameter of the iron band was a little less than that of the wheel. This iron hoop would expand when heated and go down easily over the rim of the wheel, then when it was quickly cooled it contracted, tightening the wheel together. To measure the new band for the blacksmith, who made it, the carpenter had an instrument like a large disc which he ran around the rim. It was called a traveller.

To heat or 'redden' the iron band a great fire was put down. While this was lighting the band was placed on stones to lift it about six inches from the ground. When the fire was red, the hot coals were heaped around the band in a circle of fire. More turf was added and in time you could see the red ring inside the fire. Many neighbours came to see the operation. A fire is always an attraction. The wheel was flat on the ground, an indentation made to receive the jutting stock. When the band was red-hot, men with hay forks helped my father lift it from the fire. As the white-red band hit the air you could see thousands of little white stars winking all round the circumference. The band was held directly over the wheel and gradually lowered into position. As the hot iron touched the rim, white-blue smoke shot up, the hay forks were thrown away and with hammers the band was put in place. No delays now as the iron would burn too much into the wood. Buckets of water were dashed on the rim and the hot iron bubbled and sizzled. White steam came up in a burst to mingle with the white-blue smoke of the wood. As the band cooled it tightened its grip on the wheel. You could hear the crackle of the felloes as they came together and of the spokes as they sank a little deeper into the stock. The fire was put out and my father bowled the newly shod wheel up the road to the workshop. The water spilling on the oak acid of the spokes stained them black.

The wheel wasn't finished yet. The centre of the stock had to be chiselled out to take the metal box which encased the axle. The box was a cleverly thought-out affair, narrower on the outside so that the pressure of the axle tightened it in the stock. There were two ridges left proud on the outer surface, which ensured that it could not twist in the stock. It was wrapped in jute and driven home with a sledge. Now a chase was chiselled out in the front of the stock where the axle protruded to take the lynchpin. A band of iron was put inside and outside on the stock and when the wheel was painted with red lead these bands and the edge of the big band were touched in black paint. More black in the chase and the wheel was complete. When my father made a cart the finished article was painted the same colour as the wheels, and all the ironwork, boltheads and so on in black, with a pair of guards in a shade of Reckett's Blue. If you made it yourself you would stay up all night looking at it!

II

THE HANDS OF WAR

My first faltering steps I heard about from my mother. I stood in the field, she often said, wavered a little and then stumbled three paces into her outstretched arms. She was sitting on the grass playing 'gobs'. She hadn't yet forgotten the games of her schooldays. To play you used five pebbles the size of a robin's egg. You put four pebbles down, marking the four corners of a square with the fifth in the middle. You threw up the middle one and tried to pick up as many of the others before you caught the first one falling. The person who could pick up the four on the ground before the first one fell into her hand was very expert. My mother added a complication to the game by catching the falling pebbles on the back of her open hand.

I didn't wear trousers at first. I walked around in petti-coats, as did all the male children until they were three or four. The petticoat was a sensible enough form of attire as with little training I could perform the minor call of nature without wetting myself. I was able to carry out the natural functions in a manly fashion before I stuck my legs into a trousers. I remember the occasion: the little pants came to just above my knees. But the longest memory in my head is of sitting in my father's lap — I can still smell the tobacco from his waistcoat — and fitting on a pair of shoes my aunt sent me from America. When my father put me standing I stamped and stamped my feet on the floor, fascinated by the noise I made.

When my brother was born about two and a half years after me I wasn't the centre of attention any more, and I moved out of the kitchen and spent more time in the workshop. My father had his work cut out for him to keep me away from the sharp tools. He made a small wooden hammer for me and gave me pieces of wood to play with. I sat in the shavings and listened to the men who came with jobs for my father. They all spoke to me and those who knew my grandfather were surprised that I wasn't called after him. The custom then was to call the first son after his father's father and the second son after his mother's father. The same rule applied to the first two girls. They were called after their grandmothers. If you walked into a house at that time and there were two boys and two girls in the family and you knew their grandparents, you could name the children. Both my male grandparents, who were inseparable friends, objected to my father's and mother's marriage. They claimed there was a blood relationship, though fairly far out, and the slightest trace of consanguinity had to be avoided. My mother was very upset by this attitude and called me after my father to annoy the old man. My father's Christian name was Edmund, Ned to everybody, and so was I.

Years after, as a young carpenter's apprentice, I worked with my father on the building of Clifford's Hotel in town. Old John Clifford became confused because when he called me my father used to answer, and when he called my father I often replied, 'Yes, John!' He decided to call me Éamon but the name never stuck; at home and to my neighbours I was always Ned.

The house I came to as a child was a rural cottage with a slate roof. Slate roofs were rare then; all our neighbours' houses were thatched with straw and had but two rooms and an enormous kitchen. By comparison our kitchen was small but we had three rooms. The kitchen had an open fireplace not as big as the fireplaces in the farmers' houses but big enough to seat a large company around it when in winter our house became a visiting place, what was known in our district as a rambling house. The stairs went up from the kitchen to the two rooms overhead, and now that I had got over the crawling stage and was able to walk, climbing the stairs became my greatest ambition. My mother, dreading that I would fall, often rescued me from the third or fourth step. A chair was placed at the bottom to impede my passage but this created the danger that I could pull it down on top of me. This problem was solved by my father making a small door bolted on the inside to the newel post, and that door remained in position until the family, all eight of us, grew up.

The kitchen floor had 12"x12" fireclay tiles. Concrete hadn't yet become a popular floor-making material. A big turf fire burned in the hearth, making the men who came at night push back their chairs. All the men smoked pipes and pipe smoking induced spitting, hence the spittoons and sawdust on public house floors. One of our visitors who had two lower front teeth missing could manipulate a spit, triggering it with his tongue and sending it soaring through the air in a flat parabolic curve to land on a burning coal on the hearth. His accuracy was amazing. The spit sizzled on the red coal for an instant, then the spot went black but in no time was red again until another spit landed on the same place.

When I was very small my mother put me to bed before the company came in at night. As I lay in my parents' bed I could hear the men talking below me in the kitchen. The rise and fall of the voices had a soporific effect on me and gradually I fell asleep. When I got a little older I stayed up longer and as my bedtime came I went up the stairs, my mother walking behind me in case I fell, to a chorus of 'goodnights' and '*codladh sámh*' (sound sleep) from a crowded kitchen. My mother stayed with me, telling me about 'Jackie Dorey in his red cap who went to the wood' until I fell asleep. Then she tiptoed down the stairs with a 'ssh' to the men; and all brought their voices down. Little by little the voices rose again but by this time I was far away in dreamland.

The men who rambled to our house were the married men of the locality. Some of them were old, there were a few bachelors who hadn't yet embarked on the choppy sea of matrimony, and a teenager or two. The programme for the night was varied. It started with news, worldwide and local. Those who attended fairs or markets that day had their newsy contributions to make. Men who were at a funeral or at a wake the night before started to talk about the deceased and about those who attended his obsequies. During Shrovetime there was talk of matchmaking and weddings. In times of high emigration those who had been to the railway station to see young men and women bid a fond farewell to their native place talked about our neighbours' children who had gone. They talked fondly of those who, for some time, had made their home on a foreign shore. They showed their pleasure at the news of local men who had made good and were saddened by the fact that men and women went away and were never heard of again.

War in foreign lands claimed the men's attention and as I grew a little older the Great War raged in Europe. News came to us from New York that my mother's brother, Eugene, had been drafted into the Fighting 69th contingent.

Letters came from him while he was in the training camp in Albany, and one letter when he went overseas to France. It was Eugene's last letter and it was kept in a small box with a sliding top which my father had made for my mother. The rent book was kept there and other small precious belongings of her own. When my brothers and I were a little older she would take Eugene's letter out of the box and read to us as we sat on the floor around her. He described what it was like in the trenches: the sound of the big guns noising overhead, the mud and water and rats in search of little morsels of food. 'Not far away from where I sit in this dugout,' he wrote, 'a young German soldier is taking his long last sleep, reminding me, Hannah, that unless God is very fond of me . . .' My mother, who had been holding back the tears, would cry openly and we would cry too, as much for the young German soldier as for our uncle Eugene. He never came back. He died of the great flu on 22 November 1918, eleven days after the Armistice. The American government offered to send his body home, and my grandfather spoke to his neighbours who had come to share his sorrow. One neighbour said, 'How do you know, Tim, that it is your son will be in that box?' He sowed the seeds of doubt in the old man's mind and he declined the offer. My uncle lies in an American cemetery at Meuse, Argonne, northwest of Verdun. There are neat rows of graves with white crosses and his name and his rank are on his. 'Cpl. Eugene C. Cashman, 307 Infantry, 77 Division, State of New York.'

As well as the war many is the subject the men would discuss. Politics were ever high on the agenda, the work of the Board of Guardians and the goings-on in the British Parliament where our local MP sat. 'Will I get in this time?' the sitting MP said once to one of our neighbours, coming up to polling day. 'Of course you will,' the neighbour told him. 'Didn't you say yourself that it was the poor put you in the last time and aren't there twice as many poor there now!' Sullivan and Murphy were the two contenders for the Westminster seat and their followers, the Sullivanites and the Murphyites, fought with ashplants on fair days or at sports meetings. The cries of 'Up Sullivan!' or 'Up Murphy!' echoed long into the night.

The 1918 election, with victory for Sinn Fein, put an end to that era. And on the heels of the 1918 election came the first rumblings of the War of Independence. There were echoes of the Somme and the Dardanelles nearer home now. Young Flor Donoghue, who worked at Dineens, and Mick Lynch came into our house and my mother gave them tea. Their rifles leaned against the newel post of the stairs and sitting on the floor I rubbed my hands along the polished stocks. At night when we heard the noise of the Crossley tenders coming up Mac's Height we ducked under the table as my mother's hand reached up to turn down the wick of the oil lamp. We crouched in the darkness as the Tan lorries came near the house and we held our breath until they had passed. Then as the sound died away by the Gap of the Two Sticks we gradually emerged and my mother turned up the wick of the oil lamp.

The men didn't come rambling to our house during the Tan War. A list of the occupants of the household was nailed up inside the front door. I can still see it. Parents: Edmund Kelly, Hannah Kelly. Children: Edmund Kelly, Timothy Kelly, Laurence Kelly. If anybody else was found in the house when the Tans called we would have some explaining to do. My father was one day working in the open beside the workshop. He was sawing a board and I was blowing the sawdust off the pencil line. Two English soldiers came in asking questions about who was living in the neighbouring houses. The

Daniels, the same day, were picking stones in the high field
and when the horse butt was full they heeled it into a gripe.
The loud noise of the falling stones made the soldiers spring
to attention.

'What was that?' they said, as they backed my father
against the wall. He explained what had happened and he
showed them the young boys working in the field. They went
and inspected it for themselves. If my father wasn't telling
the truth God only knows what would have happened to
him. People said that the British Tommy was a civilised
enough individual, but the Black and Tans were a murderous
crew. Many were the stories told about the burnings throughout the country. A man well known to my father and mother
— he came from where they were born — was tied to a Tan
lorry and dragged live behind it until he died; and the day
after Headford Ambush, in which twenty-three English
soldiers and two IRA men died, the Black and Tans went
through the countryside shooting anything that moved, even
the animals in the fields.

But they weren't alone in the cruelty of their ways. Two
young English soldiers deserted from the ranks. They went
into hiding and lived away from the towns until they came to
a secluded place where they worked for farmers and lived a
happy enough existence in that small community. Nothing
would convince certain elements in the IRA but that they
were spies. They were tried in their absence and sentence
was passed on them. One night the two young soldiers were
playing cards in a neighbour's house when there was a knock
at the door. Two armed men came in and despite the
pleadings of the people that the soldiers were innocent their
hands were tied behind their backs. They were blindfolded
and taken to a cowshed. The armed men wanted someone
to hold a candle in the cowhouse. The men listening made

no move. 'So much for spunk!' a woman said. 'I'll hold it myself.' Maybe the terrible story of that night expanded in the telling. By the time it reached us we were told that one young soldier asked for a priest. There was a delay in the pretence that one was being sent for, and when he arrived the blindfold was eased. The 'priest' was one of his execution-ers who had donned a black coat and placed a folded white handkerchief around his neck. Kneeling in the half-dark the frightened soldier confessed his mild transgressions that wouldn't bring a blush to the cheeks of a saint. What an obscenity! When I heard that part of the story I thought of my uncle Eugene dying far from home. What did republics or empires mean to him or to these two young men cut off from life and the love and the opportunities the future could bring? 'I must give you my address,' the young man said to the 'priest'. 'You will write to my mother?' he asked quietly. The other soldier kept his silence. He never groaned or cried out but went to his death without a word. They were buried, half-alive some claimed, in the bog.

I thought of the animals in that cowshed and I wondered did the cows jump with fright when the shots rang out, or did one cow give a low moan of agony as a cow often does when she is bringing her calf into the world.

The truce came. I was seven years old and helping the Daniels with the hay in the *leaca* field. It was a July day and the lorries of British soldiers drove up and down Boher Vass. They sang and cheered and waved to us and we small people waved back to them. The men came again and sat in our kitchen, and when the subject of the two young soldiers came down, one man said of the armed men who perpet-rated that awful atrocity, 'They will melt,' he said, 'like the froth in the river!' Bloodstains remained on the walls of the cowshed. No water could wash them off.

III

FIGHTING AMONG OURSELVES

I was over seven years of age when I went to school in the autumn of 1921. I was always a delicate child and my mother thought she'd never rear me. She swore by beef tea and chicken broth as body builders, but the sustenance failed to fill out my spare shanks.

Molly and Nell Murphy called for me that first morning. They were a few years older than me. My mother held back the tears as I went out the front door in a navy suit, Eton collar and no shoes. All the scholars went barefoot until the winter months.

'How old are you, Edmund?' Mrs O'Leary, the school-mistress, asked me. Jerry Mac, Jer Daniels and Con Dineen nearly burst out laughing when they heard her calling me Edmund. To them and everyone at home I was Ned, young Ned. 'How old are you, Edmund?' she said again.

'I am seven years since last March,' I replied.

'And why did it take so long for you to come to school, Edmund?'

'Well the way it was, Ma'am,' I said, settling myself and talking like one of the men in my father's rambling house. 'The way it was, we were every day waiting for the Tan war to be over!'

'Now that you are here, Edmund,' she told me, 'you'll have to learn very fast to make up for lost time.' And she gave me a new penny. My mother had taught me how to count up to twenty, and I knew most of the letters of the alphabet. Indeed I recognised words like 'cat' and three-lettered words in a sentence like, 'Ned put his leg in the tub.' I had a little head start and I made good progress.

As the autumn died and the winter came, a fire was lit in the school. The pupils supplied the fuel. Well-to-do farmers brought a creel of turf, heeled it out at the gate and boys in the big classes brought it in the armfuls and put it in the turf box in the hall. Those of us who couldn't afford to bring fuel by the creel brought a sod of turf to school each morning. My mother went through the turf shed to find a small sod for me.

With my mother looking after me at home, the two Murphy girls taking me to school and Mrs O'Leary's daughter teaching me, I began to feel that I was too much under petticoat rule. Having so many women around me was bad for my image. I made friends fast with boys of my own age and even though of a shy nature I managed to get into a few fights. In the playground one day I got a puck of a fist into the throat, sinking the big stud of the Eton collar into my Adam's apple. I cried from pain but soon dried my tears. That belt of a fist hardened me. I left the house on my own every morning and sought the company of the boys going and coming from school. I never again sat down with the girls as they played the game of gobs on the grassy patch by Mac's Well.

Older brothers of the boys going to school were out in the IRA. Not yet carrying arms, they acted as scouts, and one morning we saw Jimmy Williams with a spyglass scanning the countryside. He wasn't on the lookout for English troops. It was 1922 and the Civil War was on. That war divided neighbours. In one case it divided a household as two brothers fought on opposite sides. And it divided us school-children. In the playground and on the way home from school we fought the Republican and the Free State cause. I was on the Republican side. I didn't know what it meant. All I knew was that my Uncle Larry, who worked in Dublin, was a prisoner of the Free State Government and was on hunger strike.

We fought with our fists. We squared out in front of an opponent and called, 'Come on! Put up the dukes!' and the boy who couldn't keep his guard ended up with a bloodied nose. Boys whose fathers accepted the Treaty called us Republicans murderers and looters. And looting did go on. The men talked about it around my father's fire. They told of a prominent citizen who took a cartload of furniture out of the Great Southern Hotel before it was taken over by the regular army. He unloaded his booty in a laneway off College Street and went back to the hotel for a second load. When he returned to College Street the first load was gone. Lifting his eyes to heaven he shouted to the clouds, 'This town is nothing but the seed and breed of robbers! A man couldn't leave anything out of his hand!'

Running battles took place along the road when we were freed from school. Opposing armies lined up and threw stones and clods of earth at each other. The Dineens and I soon found that our Republican allies deserted us, not through cowardice, but because of the fact that they had reached their homes. Now that we were greatly outnumbered by Free State forces, we had to leg it out of the firing line, and take the short-cut home through Mick Sullivan's fields.

But our schoolboy war came to an end when we were

brought face to face with the real thing. One day when we were out to play, two Republican soldiers, young Mick Sullivan and Dinny Connor, passed by the school. I can still see their gaitered legs, the rifles slung from their shoulders and the bandoliers about their breasts. One wore a hat and the other a cap. They didn't slope along. They walked as if they were marching to music. The big boys out of fifth and sixth classes walked along with them, chatting all the while. 'We heard shots,' the big boys said. 'The military are some-where near.' 'That firing,' one of the men replied, 'is as far away as Millstreet.' We watched them as they passed by Jer Leary's house until they were out of sight around the bend towards Fordes' cottage.

Playtime over, the bell rang for us to go back to the classroom. Some time afterwards we heard gunfire, then the sound of lorries. Standing on a desk and looking out, one of the boys said there were soldiers everywhere. It seems when the two Republicans had got around the bend out of our view they looked down into the village of Knockanes and saw that the place was full of military. They decided to engage them and fired into the village. If the soldiers advanced they could easily retreat. They were local men and knew the countryside. Advance the soldiers did, and some say that, hiding behind fences, they put their caps on the tops of their rifles to draw the Irregulars' fire, while others fanned out to encircle the two men. Realising that they could soon be trapped, Connor and Sullivan split up and made a dash for it. In the getaway Mick Sullivan was wounded in the arm. Dinny Connor made his escape and Sullivan barely made it to Jer Leary's house. The Free State advance party was there as soon. Because of his wounded arm Mick Sullivan couldn't use his gun. The soldiers burst into the kitchen. Sullivan surrendered but despite the protests of Jer Leary and his wife they dragged

Mick Sullivan outside the front door and shot him dead.

When news came to the school that he was shot, the school missus and her daughter, later Mrs Spillane, were overcome with grief. We, seeing the anguish in their faces, tried to hold back the tears, and the big girls in the upper classes cried openly. It was then I saw my first Free State soldier. He came into the classroom and stood under the clock. He was a doctor. He wore a white coat which was open at the front and we could see his uniform and his Sam Browne belt. He spoke to Mrs O'Leary very quietly. As far as we could make out he said there was no need to be afraid, that the fighting was over. When he went out we heard the lorries going away. We knelt down and prayed for the soul of the young man lying dead two doors away. In a while's time, as no one could settle down to work again, the school was closed and we went home.

There was no stone-throwing on the road that afternoon. We went quietly and told our parents of the dreadful happening. 'You are too young,' my mother said, 'to be a witness to such terrible things.' I was put to bed early that night and when I came down in the morning there on the window-sill I saw a clay pipe and I knew that my father had spent the night at young Mick Sullivan's wake. The men sitting at our fireside talked the next night and for many a night about the shooting and the refusal of the parish priest to come and give the last rites to the man who died.

Other nights brought other stories. Young Republicans in Kenmare climbed a lean-to roof in the night time, entered a bedroom and shot dead two Free State soldiers as they slept. They were brothers, killed in their father's house when they were home on furlough. Stories of horror vied with each other for our attention: the blowing up of Republican prisoners at Ballyseedy, and forever etched in our minds remains the image of Dave Nelligan, a military officer, taking off his cap and combing his hair as he walked down Fair Hill in Killarney at the head of his troops after they had blown to pieces young Republicans on a mined barricade at the Countess Bridge.

The Civil War was a black time. It blackened the people's minds. Neighbours disagreed as they followed their different loyalties. Old feuds, long dead, were reopened and hatred was the prevailing emotion. Men in Tralee who were being given back the dead body of a Republican by the regular army refused to accept the remains in a Free State coffin. They went down the town and brought a new one, and with hatchets smashed to pieces the coffin in which he had lain.

Our parish priest, who had refused the last rites to Mick Sullivan, preached continually against the Irregular soldiers. One Sunday he lit the church with language. So fiery was his condemnation of what he called looters and murderers that men of the same way of thinking as Mick Sullivan and Dinny Connor rose from their seats in the body of the church and walked out. A loose heeltip went clanging at every second step on the tiles of the aisle, as if in protest against the reviling of the Republican cause.

IV

GOING AWAY AND STAYING AT HOME

When I was very small I walked down Bohar Vass with my father, out under the railway bridge and along the road leading to the Iron Mills. We were hand in hand, my chubby fist holding on to his little finger. He was in his good clothes. It was Sunday and it was the first time I remember being alone with him outside the workshop. The signal pole gleaming white on the railway line attracted my attention. He explained how it worked. The red arm up to stop the train, and down when the way was free of danger. At night when the arm was up there was a red light and when it was down the light was green. Every night Jackie Ryan put a lighting lantern inside the glass.

A train came. Quite suddenly it appeared and the loud whistle frightened me. Smoke puffed from its chimney and steam hissed from all over the engine like the kettle boiling over the fire. In the blinking of an eye it flew past with a loud rattle and disappeared under an arch over the railway.

My father, with a piece of stick, drew in the sandy roadside the map of Ireland. There was no England or Europe, just Ireland with the sea all round it. With the point of the stick he indicated the towns and cities he could remember and he drew lines between the towns where the train ran. I watched the train many times before I was old enough to board it. I watched the train with Jer Daniels when his brother, Dan, and other young men were going to America. We stood in the same place where my father drew the map and watched the train as it went slowly up hill on its way to Cork and Queenstown. Dan lowered the window and waved to us and we waved to him. We said goodbye and he shouted to us but we couldn't make out what he said because of the noise of the train. Jer Daniels cried after his brother. He had his big dog Shep with him and the dog, excited by Jer's crying, jumped up and put his paws on Jer's shoulders. With Jer's arms around him they both fell to the ground, Jer roaring crying and the dog licking the tears from his face.

The night before had been the American wake. Those going away and their friends came to one house where there was music, dancing and songs, sad and merry. I had learned a song from a gramophone that had come to Murphys' from America; a victrola the Yanks called the gramophone. That night, young as I was, I sang the song which opened with the line 'From this valley they say you are going'. When the music struck up the young emigrants danced with spirit, pounding the flags as if to vent the sorrow of parting on the kitchen floor, while the light from the oil lamp cast their dancing shadows around the whitewashed walls. By the fire the older people sat, fathers and mothers of those going away. The red glow from the fire lit their features as they kept time to the music with their feet. A mother, watching her fine son stepping it out, suddenly turned her face to the fire and watched the dancing flames as his young life up to that moment unfolded before her eyes.

Some emigrants danced throughout the night until it was time to go to the railway station in the morning. A line of horse-drawn cars, traps and sidecars then set out in time for people to have a drink in town and so that the mothers could buy a present for a departing son or daughter. It was usual to give a crown piece as a keepsake or a half-sovereign, and happy would be the one who got a golden guinea. As well as that, a present of wearables, gloves or the like, would be given to the girls, and the men got a silk handkerchief. It was sometimes thrown at the wall and if it clung to the mortar it was the genuine article. Those handkerchiefs waved from the train as it disappeared under the Countess Bridge.

Emigrants were lonesome leaving their own house and Paddy Murphy went back and opened the door and had one last look inside. I was old enough to be allowed go to the railway station that day. The train from Tralee ran out the Cork line and then reversed into the platform, where the young people going away were surrounded by their friends. It took eight to ten days to get to America in rickety old ships. You could feel the motion of the waves under your feet. A young man landing in New York had to work hard to put the passage money together to bring out his brother. That's how it was done. John brought out Tim and Tim brought out Mary. Maybe then the young man would get married and have responsibilities so when again would he have the money to come back over the great hump of the ocean? Now he stood for the last time among his relations. He started saying goodbye at the outside of the circle to his neighbours, his uncles, aunts and cousins, full of gab for everyone. But as he came to the centre the flow of words deserted him and it was only with a whispering of names that he said farewell to his brothers and sisters. His father held his hand, not wanting to let it go, and his mother, whom he had left until last, threw her arms around him, a thing she hadn't done since he was a small boy going to school, and gave vent to a cry that was taken up by the other women along the platform.

Oh, it was a terrifying thing for one as young as me to hear, and that cry used to have an effect even on older people. Nora Kissane told me she once saw a man race down the platform after the departing train so demented that he shook his fist at the engine and shouted, 'Bad luck to you oul' smoky hole taking away my fine daughter from me!' When those who were leaving boarded the train and put down the windows, their dear ones still held on to them, and when the train pulled out they were dragged along the platform until they had to let go. Some mothers collapsed on their knees under the great weight of loneliness and had to be helped to their feet, but the train gathered speed and the silk handkerchiefs waving from the windows was the last sight of them we saw.

> They travelled on for fifteen miles
> By the banks of the River Lee.
> Spike Island soon came into view,
> And the convicts they did see.
> They all put up in Mackey's Hotel
> Nine dozen of them and more,
> And they sang and danced the whole night long,
> As they did the night before.

In the morning they went out in the tender to the waiting ship and sailed away. The first letters to come from them came from mid-Atlantic. It seems that east- and west-bound liners drew alongside and mail was exchanged. The letters told of their night's stay in Queenstown and of their first days at sea. They were poor sailors and try as they might they couldn't keep the food down. Their time was spent at the ship's rail retching emptily into the sea. The half-circle of white foam at the base of Sceilig Mhichíl was their last glimpse of Ireland. They promised to write when they had settled in America and when they got work they would send some money.

At home many families were reduced by half. But life went on. The tasks had to be done. Cows had to be milked, calves fed and the eggs brought in from the rogue hen's nest. The seasons brought different work to the community that lived around us and the first activity of the year was the setting of the potato garden. A large field went with our house. My father ran a wire fence through it, north to south. One part was known as East the Wire and the other as West the Wire. East the Wire was the smaller of the divisions, and here in the spring, if it had been under grass the year before, ridges were formed. These ridges my father, and maybe a helper, made with a spade. The spade was the implement of the strolling labourers of old. Eoghan Ruadh the poet worked with one and ridged a garden as he composed his songs, as far away from home as Cork and Limerick. The spade, made originally by the smith and later at Scott's foundry in Cork, had a sharp edge and a long handle and a treader. The operator cut the sod and turned it over, grassy side down, leaving a furrow as he worked along.

The ridges when completed with the spade looked a neat piece of handiwork and a furrow between each two ridges ran the entire length of the allotment. My father 'threw his eye' along the furrow and said with some satisfaction, 'As straight as a dye!' Each eye in a potato will sprout a shoot and as all that was needed was one stalk, the potato was cut into pieces, each piece holding at least one eye. The work of cutting the potatoes was done by women. They came to each other's houses and worked together, sitting on chairs in the kitchen. They talked, ribbed each other about their men, told stories and were high good company. My job as a child was keeping them supplied with whole potatoes and taking away the eyeless waste pieces which were boiled and given to the pigs. The precious small piece holding an eye and maybe a young shoot was called a *sciollán*. There were many things in our district for which there was no English word and that was one. Fresh lime was shaken on the sciollauns to keep them from bleeding.

The planting on the ridges was done with the spade. His foot on the treader, the sower drove the spade deep into the ridge. Then, thrusting it forward and releasing it, he left a gaping hole. Into this the sciollaun was flung from a home-made jute satchel which the sower wore around his shoulders. Each ridge carried three rows. I had the choice of two jobs when I was strong enough to be of help. One was to hold the satchel and shoot a sciollaun into the hole as my father made it. The other was to strike down the sod on the gaping holes. I often ended up doing both.

There was a manure heap in the yard outside the cowshed on which the droppings of the animals were piled. To this, refuse from the kitchen was added. The manure was drawn out in the pony cart or in a creel basket and spread on the ridges. There was bag manure shaken on top called guano. This was the excrement of sea birds which came from the islands off Peru. I laughed to think that the droppings of colourful birds from South America mingling with the droppings of our hens and those of the cow and the pony helped grow our potatoes. With the spade we dug the earth in the furrows and with a shovel this earth was used to cover the manure on the ridges. Later on, when the stalks appeared and grew a few inches, the furrows were dug again and the soil, called second earthing, was distributed between the stalks.

It was an anxious time when the stalks were at this tender stage. A late frost could burn them up and all our work was gone for nothing. If the frost came my father was up before the dawn and with a piece of broom or a bunch of ferns or heather he would brush the frost crystals from the stalk leaves before the sun shone on them. The potato was an important item of food — king of the menu as one poet said — and the progress of the gardens was a topic of conversation in our rambling house at night. The men talked about the varieties of potato and the preference of different varieties for different soils. The Champion, all agreed, liked boggy ground. Potatoes from this type of soil were so clean when dug that they could be put in the pot without washing them.

Another anxiety for the people was the potato blight, which left the potatoes rotten in the fields in Black '47. When the stalks were high and closing in over the furrows, humid weather brought this dreaded disease. To guard against it the crop was sprayed. That day was a big day for me. I was kept in from school to help my father. We tackled the pony, a recent acquisition called Fanny, to the car and brought water from the river in an old wine barrel of which there was a few in every house. A second barrel was on the headland and the water in the barrel in the pony car was transferred to it. Bluestone and washing soda in certain proportions were put steeping the night before and when melted down were added to the barrel of water on the headland to make a bluish-green liquid. The back-board of the butt was placed on the barrel, not covering it fully, and the knapsack spraying machine rested on it.

This machine, to my young eyes, was an absolute marvel. It belonged to the shopkeeper who sold the bluestone and washing soda and was given free to his customers. It was about twenty inches square and about eight inches deep. The cover at the top had a rubber seal and with a little lever it clamped down tight when the tank was full. There was a handle at the right hand side and at the left a length of hose attached to a pipe, at the end of which was a rose head like that on a watering can. The sprayer was hollowed on one side to fit on the operator's back. When the tank had its quota of green-blue liquid and the cover was secured tightly, my father put his back to it and adjusted the straps that came over his shoulders. First he worked the handle at the right hand side up and down with a vigorous motion, pumping air into the liquid, and when he felt he had a good head up he released the tap on the pipe in his left hand and out shot a spray, making a sizzling sound. It was so concentrated that, as it came from the rose head, it turned into a cloud of vapour. He walked through a furrow, spraying a ridge at each side of him and as the spray dried on the stalks the dark green garden turned a bluish-green under the heat of the sun. When he returned with an empty tank I filled it with an old saucepan. Indeed my father could have done this himself but he liked company when he was working out of doors. We didn't talk very much but we enjoyed being together. Before he finished, with the tank just a quarter full, he let me put it on my back. Even at a quarter full the weight nearly knocked me down, but I struggled on, and working the handle I pumped in the air and released the spray. I got a great kick out of the feeling of power I had over the thing as I walked the furrow, my head barely above the stalks.

New potatoes were a special delicacy. The first meal was always on a Sunday in late summer. I loved the very small ones so clean and white they didn't need to be peeled. I put a knob of butter on top which melted and ran down the sides like lava down the sides of Vesuvius as the potato made its way from the plate to my mouth. It was a special day and as we made the sign of the cross we prayed that we all might be alive this time the next year. We thanked God for the crop and for the fact that there was no repeat of Black '47.

My Aunt Bridgie often talked about the famine and what happened to the people at that time. She told a story of little children weak with hunger tugging at their mothers' skirts and asking her to put down the potatoes. To keep them from crying, when they weren't watching she put small stones in a pot with water and hung the pot over the fire. The children sat on the floor, their eyes glued to the pot, and when they thought the potatoes should be cooked they kept imploring their mother to take them up. In the end, distracted from their pleadings and weak with hunger herself, she prayed to the Blessed Virgin to intercede with the Almighty to come to her aid. She took the cover off the pot and there to gladden the hearts of herself and the children were cooked potatoes. To a child's imagination everything is possible, but I caught my father winking at my mother and I hoped my Aunt Bridgie didn't see him.

Though my Aunt Bridgie was old she didn't remember the great famine but as a child she had heard older people talk about it. She described a house to us where distant relations of our own lived in Glounacoppal. The family lay on the kitchen floor too far gone from hunger to stand up. The father and mother had watched the younger children die one by one. He decided he would try again to find some sustenance for his wife and only surviving son. A raw turnip, maybe half-hidden and forgotten in the garden, or dandelion roots which he could dig up with his fingers. He crawled out of the house and was later found dead in a field clutching a bunch of dandelion roots in his hand.

Because of these memories there was always a deep respect for food in our house. Nothing was wasted. Not a single morsel was ever thrown out. What was left over was carefully gathered and added to the mess for the hens or the pigs. A beggar never went empty-handed from a door in our neighbourhood while there was food in the house, and my mother's most fervent request of God when we knelt at our prayers was, 'Feed the hungry!'

When the potato garden faded from dark green to brown and the ageing process had continued until the stalks were white and withered, the spuds were fit to dig. The same spade which was used for the sowing helped to reap the harvest. With his foot on the treader, my father drove the spade deep under the stalk and upturned the earth, revealing eight to a dozen potatoes. I marvelled at the bounty of nature that from one small shoot so many tubers could come. With the tip of the spade my father pitched them into a row as he went and we small people and my mother picked them and put them into buckets. For the winter the potatoes were stored in a pit in the garden. A trench about a foot deep was dug and into this the tubers were put and made into a small rick coming to a point. The neat heap was covered with withered stalks collected for the purpose and finally earthed over until the pit looked like the hipped roof of a long house. There the pit remained, the contents safe from winter frost. One end was opened when a supply was wanted for the table or to feed the animals. Farmers' sons, who were unpaid, raided their fathers' pits and sold a sack of potatoes so they could get pocket money coming up to Christmas.

In the potato garden there was room for an allotment for growing cabbages and a bed or two of onions. The cabbage plants were bought in bundles of a hundred in the town market and planted in neat rows with a generous helping of manure. The plants lay in the ground withered and forlorn-looking for a while. Then they perked up and grew with a fairish rapidity until in the middle of each plant the leaves hugged together to form the beginnings of a white head. While the plant was still growing the outside leaves were plucked and broken between the bands into a tub, topped with a mess of Indian meal and fed to the cow while she was being milked.

A cabbage leaf was used as a wrapper. When our cow was dry often we found a pound of butter in a cabbage leaf on the window-sill. It was left there by a generous neighbour before we got up in the morning. Boiled cabbage was the vegetable which accompanied cured bacon on our plates.

There was an iron frame, the rack, which hung like a gate over the fire. It had hooks that could be moved along the bar. When a pot was cooked it could be shifted to the side and another pot hung on. Red coals were also put at the side of the hearth on which rested the frying pan with 'a bit of fresh thing', as my mother called meat from the butchers. The fresh thing cooked with onions we got once in a blue moon. The staple diet for the principal meal was bacon and cabbage or bacon and turnips. When you sat down to such a meal there was a mountain of laughing Murphies in the middle of the table and as that mountain went down a small mountain of potato skins rose at each elbow. There was a bowl of semi-solidified milk to wash it down and every bite that went into your mouth was produced on your own holding.

V

FOOD ON THE TABLE

The fowl had a house in the yard with a hole in the door to give them air at night. My father made a ladder-like roost for them with a stick across fairly high up for the cock to perch on so that he could preside over his harem. When the last person was going to bed at night the word was, 'Did you kindle [rake] the fire?' and 'Did you close the door on the fowl?' Our front door was never locked, not even during the Tan war, but many is the man regretted not closing his fowl house door at night. The fox was always on the prowl.

When the men at our fireside talked about animals, pride of place for cleverness was given to the fox. Many is the time I heard them tell about the farmer who had a large hole in his fowl house door. The fox squeezed himself through it and having deprecated, as the men said, his stomach swelled and he was unable to come out through the hole in the door. The fox waited until the farmer opened the door in the morning, and was that farmer surprised to see a dead fox on the floor. He took the animal by the tail and swung the lifeless body over his shoulder on his way to dump him in a gripe. When the fox got into the open air, and out of view of the dog, he nipped the farmer in the back of the leg. With a cry of pain the man let go of the tail.

It was listening to the men talking in my father's house that gave me a life-long interest in animals. I heard them describe how the fox stole honey from the wild bees' nest in a summer's meadow. Reynard sat on the nest, his thick coat of fur protecting him. The disturbed bees crawled out and the fox, putting his snout down between his hind legs, sucked the honey from the comb. One of the breed became infested with fleas, according to one of our visitors, and to get rid of them he gathered a ball of wool in his mouth from bushes near where sheep grazed. When the fox came to a lake he dipped his tail, just the tip, and with infinite patience lowered himself slowly into the water, giving the fleas plenty of time to retreat before the advancing deluge. Finally his ears were going under and then his nose and the unwanted tenants, with nowhere else to go, took refuge in the ball of wool. Suddenly, letting go the wool, the fox submerged himself, saying in his own mind, 'If that ship sinks it won't be for the want of a crew!'

Badgers and otters were often the subject of conversation. A badger, separated from his mate, will defecate while on the move. The stool, falling in a certain way, indicates to his mate which way he has gone.

But domestic animals took pride of place in the men's conversation. They were very fond of their horses and their dogs, and the women sang when milking the cows and feeding the calves. People talked to the animals as city folk talk to their pets. There was a cat in every house, not so much a pet but a working member of the family. If the dog had to mind the sheep and bring home the cattle, the cat had his work cut out for him to keep the grain loft free of rats and mice. Men boasted about the intelligence of their dogs and told exaggerated stories about their cleverness.

Stories about cats were exaggerated too. A carpenter who worked late at night trained his cat to hold a candle. The carpenter was proud of his achievement and wagered that training beats nature. A travelling man, hearing of this, laid a bet and let go a mouse in the workshop. Needless to say the cat dropped the candle and left them in the dark. Nature will out!

From the money my father earned in the workshop we were well set up in Carrigeen. By the time I went to school we had a cow and her calf, a pony, a flock of hens and a royal rooster and in the out office next to the fowl house two pigs fattening. My father bought them at the pig market when they were two small pinky-skinned *bonamhs*. He made a trough in which to feed them and we got straw for their bed. Pigs keep their bed and around where they sleep very clean and use the far end of the house for their calls of nature. My father put a half-door on the piggery so that we could look in on them. Neighbouring women passing by, having inquired about the health of the family, inquired about the animals. My mother usually brought them around to the back to see the pigs. It wasn't enough for the women to look at the two porkers; they opened the door, gave the animals a smart smack on the rump to admire them walking around, and then pronounced on how much they had improved since they last saw them. The owner of an animal likes to hear it praised and my mother was no different from anyone else.

On a summer's day my two small brothers and I loved to bring food out in the field. We would also provide some eatables for the pony, the cow and the calf and coax them to come near us while we all ate together. In our innocence we pretended that they were people. They were all tame and came quite close. The pony would eat bread and so would the cow, and when the pony grazed in Murphy's mountain we caught her by offering her bread or a handful of sugar.

The cow, when her time came, was mated with Mac's bull, for which service we paid five shillings. Neighbouring farmers, who didn't have a bull of their own, availed of the services of Mac's 'gentleman'. They paid for this by giving a day's work to the owner, and when they came together to cut Mac's turf they were known as bull men.

I was still of tender years when I took our cow to the bull. There was no one else to do it if my father was away from home except my mother, and it was considered indelicate for a woman to go on an errand like that in our community. The cow was very giddy taking her there, darting in gaps and gates, jumping on other cows and lifting her head and bellowing. I drove her into the farmyard, the owner opened the gate and then opened the stall door. When the yard gate was shut the bull came out with a ring on his nose. His belligerent appearance terrified me as he pawed the ground with his front hoof. He lifted his head high, sniffed the air and let a bloodcurdling roar out of him.

Mrs Mac, a sensitive woman, called me into the kitchen, cut a slice from a home-made cake, buttered it and shook sugar on the top and gave it to me. I was troubled because I had heard the men say at our fireside when such matters came down that to be on the safe side a bull should jump the cow three times.

'Anything bothering you?' Mrs Mac asked.

'The men always said to make sure the cow got three jumps,' I told her.

'That will be all right,' she said, 'John will see to that.'

I finished the cut of bread and put the five shillings on the table. When the cow was left out of the yard I drove her home a much quieter and more contented animal than she was coming.

When the Civil War was over and some sort of order

restored in the country, my father went off with Singleton, the contractor, rebuilding the bridges which had been blown up by the IRA during the two troubles. Singleton had a big red face and wore a broad-brimmed hat and wire-rimmed spectacles. He was always in a hurry and my father made sure he was ready when he called on Monday mornings. Singleton had an old Ford car with a canvas roof. He drove like hell and my father said that when they went over a humpbacked bridge the passengers were lifted out of their seats and their heads bounced off the canvas roof. When they were working in the Gaeltacht Singleton learned two words of Irish, *Brostaigh ort!* (Hurry on, you!), and used them to great effect on the labouring men.

My father, often I heard him describe it, made the platform which rested on the river bed, and shaped the huge mould to support the new arch. The original archstones and keystones were retrieved from the river and placed in position on the mould, and concrete was grouted down between them. The parapets were rebuilt and coped, and when the cement was set, they struck the fox wedges, the mould slipped down from the arch and in a day or two the road was opened for traffic. Local people who had to go through the river were now able to drive over the restored bridge. On Saturday nights Singleton brought my father home from places as far away as Duagh and Annascaul.

It was when my father was away that our cow — Buckley, called after the man we bought her from — decided to calf. We had watched her barrel grow bigger and bigger during the preceding months and her udder go dry. When the time came and she was in labour, I went and told my mother. She was too unwell to come downstairs as she was expecting another baby but she asked me and my younger brother, Tim, to sit by her bedside and she explained to us what we could do to help the cow have her calf.

Feeling very important we lit a candle and went out to the cowshed to sit and wait. The cow was lying down and the sign we were to watch out for was two hollows that would come on her back just above her tail. When this happened it meant that the pin bones were down and the new arrival would soon be on its way. The first thing that happened was that the water bag appeared. This was the 'blister' my mother told us to expect. That broke and the cow's behind opened very wide as the 'crubs' worked their way out. These crubs – my mother's word – were the calf's front feet. They hadn't come very far when the calf's nose came into view, resting on the feet. The nose was covered with mucus which we wiped away to give the little animal a chance to breathe. The cow looked back at us from where she was tied, giving a low moan with every stitch and with a wild look in her eyes. If the birth movement stopped, my mother told us to catch the front feet and give a gentle tug to coincide with the cow's natural ejection process. This we did and the calf came gradually into the light, his eyes shut. We heaved, holding a leg each, until all of a sudden the calf shot out, knocking the two of us back on the floor. He lay there, a slimy mess. His body was very small and when after a while he staggered to his feet he seemed all legs. His mother was pleading for him as she shivered with excitement. We coaxed him up, reeling drunkenly on his long legs, until he was under her head. She licked his face lovingly and licked his body.

We had plenty of hot water ready, to which we added bran in a tub. We placed it under the cow's head and she drank it greedily. We had to coax the calf away. He wasn't left to suckle the cow. He had to be taught to drink milk from a bucket. My father had placed the rail of the cart in the cowshed. We walked the little calf into this pen and put on the back gate. We went then and told my mother the whole story. She felt well enough to get up and milk the cow. Putting the milk in a bucket she showed us how to teach the calf to drink. She put her finger, dripping with milk, into the calf's mouth. No fear of being bitten, he had no teeth yet. He sucked the milk from her fingers as if he were sucking his mother's teat. It took him a few days to get the hang of it, but when he did he put his head in the bucket, drank what was there, and bellowed for more.

After feeding the calf there was plenty of milk left over for the use of the house, milk to colour our tea and to drink. We even managed to save some to put in a large shallow pan. In time the cream came to the top and was skimmed off with a saucer. When there was a fair quantity of cream collected it was put in a small table churn. When you twisted the handle, a ladder-like frame on the inside went through the cream. After much hard work — and everyone had to take a turn — the cream was made into butter. If you were passing a farmer's dairy on churning day it would be considered unlucky if you didn't give a hand. It was said if you purposely passed by without helping, you would take the size of your head of butter from the dairy. If you gave a hand I suppose the reverse was true. Anyway, many is the time when passing Murphys' dairy on churning day I was greeted with: 'Come here and put the size of your head in the churn!'

There were two products from the churning, butter and buttermilk. The fresh butter with just a little salt added was beautiful to taste and the buttermilk had a sweet-sour tang to it. We drank it and it was used for baking.

My mother baked all the bread for the family. It was only on a very rare occasion that shop bread made its way on to our table. My mother's soda cake was made from white flour but now and then she added Indian meal to make mixed bread. Locally this was called 'yalla buck' and steaming hot and with a plentiful spreading of fresh butter it tasted delicious. As a special treat my mother added cream when baking a white cake, and a little sugar. We loved the soft spongy bread. We cheered when we saw her reaching for the cream jug or taking two paper bags from the press, one with currants, the other with raisins, and adding the dried fruit to the small mountain of flour in the bread tray. As she tossed the flour the dark fruit turned white. When she had the flour thoroughly mixed and had added a pinch of soda, she made a hole in the middle of the heap and poured in the butter-milk, soaked the flour and kneaded the dough.

When my small sister, Eliza, Elizabeth, Betty and Bess my mother called her, was big enough to climb on a chair she loved to mess with the flour and the dough. If my mother was in a good humour she let her make a small cake. My mother's cake was round and almost a foot across. When she flattened it out in the bread tray (a *lasad* in Irish, sometimes pronounced losset) she cut the sign of the cross on the cake and put a small indentation between the four arms of the cross. Then, lifting it between both hands, she lowered the cake into the pot oven, which had been dusted with flour beforehand to keep the cake from sticking to it. She hung the oven over the fire and, placing the cover on it, she heaped red coals on the cover so that the heat to bake the cake was coming from above and below. Now and again she would lift the cover slightly to see if the cake was rising. When it was baked she took the cover off and a cloud of steam went up, filling the kitchen with the aroma of freshly baked bread. The cat sat up and twitched her nostrils sideways she found the smell so good. The new cake, covered in a piece of cloth, was put on the window-sill to cool. When my mother was in high good humour she would let my little sister put her small cake in an old metal saucepan with the cover on. The coals were piled on top and it baked at the side of the fire.

Many is the hour we gave on our knees in the field gathering *caisearbhán*. This was the dandelion plant. With strong knives we levered it up from the roots. My mother put her collection in her apron, and we small people had a bucket. This heap of greenery with orange roots was put on the kitchen table, chopped up very small and added to the hens' feed and the pigs' mess. With the care they got, the pigs fattened quickly. Sometimes they were let out for exercise. They grunted and made loud throaty noises as they enjoyed their freedom. If there was a muddy pool they rolled themselves in it and then started to root up the field in search of roots or whatever it is pigs find under the sod. It was amazing the amount of ground they turned up in a short time, but they were halted in their work of turning a green field black by having their noses ringed. A neighbour would do this for us. He had an implement like a pliers into which he put an open ring with two sharp ends. With a quick movement he clamped the ring shut through the soft flesh of the pig's snout. There was a loud squeal and a little blood came as the pigs ran off, but they rooted no more.

As the pigs got very fat and lay on their straw bed, I sometimes went in and sat between them. They seemed to like having their backs scratched and when a pig's hind foot was unable, because of his fatness, to reach a certain part of his body, I scratched the itchy place with my toe. This seemed to bring him immense pleasure. But the day would come when we would have to part company, for one pig would have to go to the market and the other would find his way into the pickling tub. When I was big enough I went with my father to sell one of the pigs in town. We were up at an unearthly hour that morning. Fanny the mare was tackled and the turf rail put on the car with the back gate taken out. A pig's big floppy ears made for a great hold. I grasped his left ear in my left hand and my father his right ear with his right hand. Then we reached under the pig's barrel and grasped our hands firmly and with a one, two, three, lifted the pig and walked him into the body of the car and put on the back gate.

We climbed in ourselves and my mother brought the holy water, as she always did when we were about to set out on a journey. She shook the water on us and the mare crinkled the skin on her back as the drops fell unexpectedly on her. The pig took no notice and as my father blessed himself we began our journey. Other cars on the same errand came out gates and out the mouths of boreens and on to the main road to join us. As we neared the town the road was black with traffic and the air filled with the squealing of pigs. When we reached the fair field on Martyr's Hill, the animals had to be taken out of the cars and walked around for the jobbers to see. I had my work cut out for me to keep our pig from getting mixed up with our neighbours' livestock or straying among the town pigs which were being walked to market. Each town animal had a rope tied to one of his hind legs and his owner had a light switch with which to tap the pig on the shoulder to steer him left or right. Many people in the town's laneways kept pigs at the backs of their small houses and collected swill at the hotels and lodging houses to feed them.

When the jobbers arrived there was a murmur of anticipation among the men. What would prices be like? The jobbers wore peaked caps and brown leather gaiters over strong boots and trenchcoats not unlike the uniform of the anti-treaty IRA. One of them walked around our pig, gave him a slap of the palm of his hand and said, 'What weight is he?'

'I suppose,' my father replied, 'he'd be shoving up to a

hundred and three quarters.'

'What are you asking for him?'

'Nine pounds ten,' my father said with some conviction.

The jobber walked away as if he had been insulted. Other owners nearby had a similar experience and the feeling was that prices were down. My father brought his opening gambit down to eight pounds seventeen and sixpence when the next jobber came and after a bit of banter he too walked away.

'Don't come down any more, Ned,' a neighbour advised my father. 'You have a nice animal there. Don't let him go for nothing. Hold out!'

When the next jobber came around he asked my father, 'Are you selling the pig?'

'No,' my father said, 'I am taking him to Ballybunion on his holidays!'

The jobber and the men standing there laughed at that and the jobber and my father got talking.

'Aren't you the man,' the jobber said, 'that built the Tower Bridge on the road to Moll's Gap?'

My father admitted that he was. More conversation until the jobber said, 'Come on, the day is going,' and he offered a price for the pig. My father named his. The jobber went up a few shillings and my father came down as many more. The jobber walked away, came back and went up a few bob. My father came down a few. The jobber made his last offer and put out his hand, which my father refused. After some more talk, a neighbour intervened. 'What's between ye?'

'Ten shillings,' the jobber told him.

'Look,' says the neighbour. 'In the name of all that's high and holy split the difference.'

That was the final word. My father spit on his palm and the jobber spit on his and they shook hands on the deal. The pig went for eight pounds and five shillings. My father was satisfied. He had got what he considered was enough drama out of the scene. The pig jobber wrote a docket from the book he had in the pocket of his trenchcoat. That would be honoured in a public house later. Then with his penknife he cut his mark on the pig's rump. The pig squealed. I watched the spot where the knife had cut and after a while drops of blood oozed out, making the mark indelible. The pig had to be lifted up and put back in the car. We drove to the railway station, where he was loaded on to a wagon with the jobber's name on it. With a grunt he ran up the ramp and in no time he was lost among the other pigs. We tied the pony to the courthouse railings, gave her some hay, and I went with my father to Carthy Dennehy's public house where the jobber was paying out. He remembered my father.

'Oh ho,' he said, 'London Bridge is falling down, but not the one on the road to Moll's Gap!'

My father gave me a half-crown and called for lemonade for me. While the men talked over their drinks I walked out in the street and with a two-shilling piece my mother had given me in the morning I had a lot of money in my pocket. I went to Maggie Courtney's to buy sweets to bring home to those younger than me, and a currant cake I knew my mother would like. I didn't want to wander too far in case I got lost. I stopped to watch the sale of young pigs, pinky little *bonamhs*. They were in railed carts by the side of the street and in front of Dinny Sir John's. In some carts they were lying down and snuggled into each other, very tired after their long journey to town. Men who had sold grown pigs that morning were now buying young ones to fatten and so the cycle began again. When a little *bonamh* was bought, and the same bargaining had gone on as I had seen in the pig market, it was lifted out by the ears and transferred to the purchaser's cart. Sometimes a farmer cradled the small pig in his arms like a baby. There was much lamenting as the little fellow was parted from his comrades.

When I got back to Carthy Dennehy's public house my father and the men, having downed a few drinks, were in good order. Men drank a whiskey first and then a pint of stout. Some drank the pint first and the whiskey followed as a chaser. On a very cold morning I heard it said older men called for two whiskeys, drank one and poured the other into their boots to warm their feet. In a while's time my father tore himself away from the company and we went to get the messages for my mother. When we got back to the court-house railing the pony was glad to see us. She gave a neigh of welcome. We stood into the rail and she hurried home.

When we sat down to our meal, all the talk was about the market. My mother was pleased enough with the price my father got for the pig. He fished it out of his pocket and gave it to her and I knew it would find its way into the box with the sliding top. She wanted to hear any news we brought. Did we see anyone she knew? She was particularly interested to hear if we had spoken to any of her relations. I had news for her about the prices young *bonambs* were making as I knew by next market day we would have space in our pigs' house for two new occupants. Then the big question was decided: the day was named for killing the pig we had kept.

When that day came, water was being boiled from an early hour. A wine barrel, not the one we used for spraying the potatoes, was cleaned out, and when the time came this was more than half-filled with scalding water. The pig butcher came, and two neighbours to help my father hold down the pig. The kitchen table was brought out in the yard and placed so that it was on a slight incline. A small noose was put at the end of a rope and the men opening the pig house door slipped the noose into the pig's mouth and tightened it over his upper jaw. He was led out to the yard, protesting loudly, and with a quick movement the men knocked him on the flat of his back on the table, his head where the table was lowest, and with a tight grip on his four legs they held him down. Pat Murrell, our next door neighbour, a pig butcher with a reputation of being quick to dispatch, had his coat off and his sleeves folded above his elbows. He took the gleaming butcher's knife so sharp it would nearly split a hair, and shaved the bristles along the pig's throat. He made a long lengthwise cut in the throat and when the flesh parted for a second it remained as clean as if he had cut a piece of cheese. Then the blood oozed out in little bubbles. My mother and small sister ran East the Wire to be out of earshot of the bloodcurdling squeals of the pig. With a swift movement Pat plunged the knife through the gash and his arm followed it to the pig's heart. The blood rushed out, the pig's voice gurgling through it, and into a large pan which I held. I was terrified to have to do it, but I wasn't prepared to appear cowardly before the neighbouring men. The pig's body was eased down the inclined table until his head hung over the edge. The butcher, his arm red like Crobh Dearg the pagan priest at The City, shouted instructions to the men to sway the body backwards and forwards and to keep moving the legs to get out all the blood. In the end the big pan was nearly full of red blood, with the last trickle of a slightly darker colour.

The barrel of scalding water was near the table and the pig was eased head first into it and worked up and down by the hind legs. Then he was pulled out and the other end was let slide into the barrel. When the boiling water had done its job of softening the bristly hair the carcass was hauled on to the table and the butcher began to shave the hairs from the skin. The men got what sharp knives were in the kitchen to help and I lent a hand myself.

When the carcass was clean the butcher removed the cloven hoof coverings from the feet, and inserted a piece of rope under the tendons of the pig's hind legs to hang him from a short ladder. There was a tub under the head, which had a spud in its mouth. Now with the knife the butcher cut the pig open from his tail to his throat and all his insides slid down into the tub. The liver and heart were removed and given to my mother and I got the bladder. It was like a small balloon with little nodules of fat stuck to the outside. I squeezed it and a squirt of urine shot out. I filled it with water and washed it well and put it in the shoulder of the flue over the fire. When it was dry I would blow it up, tie a cord at the neck and invite the neighbouring lads for a game of football.

At nightfall the ladder was brought into the kitchen. The carcass was too valuable to be left outside for wild dogs to feast on. When the lamp was lit the light fell on the hanging animal. As I sat at the fire I couldn't take my eyes off him. He was sad and comical with his front held open by three sally rods and his mouth held open with a spud. If you looked at him through half-closed eyes he could be laughing or crying. Holy God! I thought what he had suffered to bring us food for the entire winter. My mother, knowing the softie I was, suspected that I would be crying myself next. She gave me a cup of hot milk and walked me up the stairs to bed. 'That's the way the world is,' she said, 'and animals were put into it for our use and benefit.' The excitement of the day kept me awake for a long time and when I went to sleep I dreamt that it was I who was killed instead of the pig. I saw my naked body hanging from the ladder with a spud in my mouth. I saw the spud falling out of my mouth and my soul coming after it and floating up through the clouds. Heaven was full of pigs. Some had wings and a very fat pig looked like Singleton the bridge builder. He was driving a car with a canvas roof. I couldn't mistake him. The same fat face under a broad-rimmed hat. He wore spectacles and had a gold ring in his nose.

Next morning the pig's intestines were taken in a tin bath to the river. I helped my mother to wash them; sometimes a neighbour's wife or daughter would also lend a hand. The running water was let flow through what seemed like miles of pig's gut and the gut was turned inside out so that it was thoroughly cleaned. The intestines were cut into lengths of from sixteen to eighteen inches, placed in the bath and brought home. where a busy day lay ahead for my mother and her helpers. Oatenmeal, milk, onions with seasoning of pepper, salt and spice were added to the pig's blood in the dish which I had held the day before. There was a big pot of boiling water over the fire. My mother took an eighteen-inch-long piece of intestine and tied one end with bageen thread. This was the thread which was saved when empty flour bags were opened out to make bed sheets and even articles of women's wear. Holding the other end of the gut open she spooned the mixture into it, and putting the spoon aside she squeezed the contents down along the intestine. When the length of gut was over three-quarters full – room was left for the pudding to expand – she tied the two ends together so that she had in her hand what looked like a small, pumped-up bicycle tube. Two or maybe three sticks were stretched over the mouth of the pot, and as my mother completed the filling of a pudding she put it in over the stick so that it hung down into the boiling water where it began to cook. She kept turning the wheels of pudding on the sticks to let the boiling water get to all of them and each one got the stab of a fork to let the air out.

When the job was ended the kitchen was full of puddings. We didn't eat them all ourselves. When God smiled on you you shared with your neighbour. It was my job to go to each neighbouring house with a dinner plate on which was a half circle of pudding and a pork steak. People were delighted to receive the gift and they would give the same to us and maybe more when God smiled on them.

When night time came there were two lamps lighting in our kitchen for the salting of the pig. The neighbouring farmer, Pat Murrell, who had killed the pig, and Daniel Moynihan came. The carcass was cut into flitches and the kitchen table was placed in the middle of the floor. My father nailed a board around three sides of it to keep the salt from falling on the floor. Two and a half stone of salt was bought that day and a little saltpetre was added to it. Each man took a flitch of meat and rubbed the salt well into it, into the skin as well as the flesh. Pockets were made in the flesh and salt stuffed in them as well as deep into the piece of meat that held a bone. The big wine barrel was placed at the bottom of the kitchen and the flitches of salted meat and the head now cut in half were firmly packed into it. When the last piece went in more salt was shaken on the meat and a large flat stone placed on top. A cloth was put over the mouth of the barrel and nine days later my father would look to see if the pickle was rising. If this liquid kept coming up until all the meat was covered the curing was a success.

In three weeks the flitches would be taken out and put hanging from the joists. They would drip for a day or two and we children avoided walking under them. It was said that if a drop fell on our heads we would go bald. But the curing process continued, with the smoke from the fire helping to mature the bacon. When our principal meal was being prepared all my mother had to do was reach for a hanging flitch and cut off what bacon she wanted for the pot, and while there were potatoes in the pit and York cabbage or turnips in the garden no one in our house went hungry.

VI

RECEIVING

When the men came at night they picked a place for their chairs so as not to be sitting under a flitch of dripping bacon. Not that a drop of brine on their heads would make any difference for they all wore hats and caps. The men never removed their headgear except when going to bed or at Mass. Indeed it was on seeing the men bareheaded in the chapel that I discovered to my surprise that many of them had not a rib of hair between them and the Almighty. White-skinned domes topped weatherbeaten faces, faces that looked very different when I saw them again with their hats on that night. Two other places I saw the men bareheaded were in the wake room, when they knelt beside the bed to pray, and at the graveside, but as soon as ever the priest had said the final prayer, a decade of the rosary, the hats and caps were on again.

The men wore their working clothes when they came rambling to our house at night. This attire was once their Sunday best. The shirt was of flannel, something like an army greyback. There was a brass stud in front and a buttonhole at the back of the collar band to take another stud. Over the shirt on Sundays they wore a starched front with a butterfly

58

collar attached. It was secured at the back and front of the shirt band with studs and was just large enough to cover the upper chest inside the waistcoat. With a necktie attached and the body coat on, it looked like a full shirt. It was as stiff as a board with starch and almost shone in its gleaming whiteness. With a navy suit, a velour hat and polished boots the wearer looked the picture of respectability going to the chapel on Sunday. But it was more the attire of the older men, and some of them as well sported a cutaway or swallow-tailed coat with two large buttons at the back. On St Patrick's Day a large spray of shamrock hung from the coat lapel and on Palm Sunday there was a sprig of palm in the hat.

My father wore a collar and tie on Sunday. The collar was starched and there often was a struggle trying to get the front and back studs through the starched clogged buttonholes. Standing on a chair I had to come to his assistance and with my tiny fingers try and force a reluctant stud through a starch-sealed hole. Somehow I succeeded and handed him the large handkerchief my mother gave me. He unfurled it, blew his nose with it and put it in his pocket. Younger men wore soft collars and many wore no collar or tie, just a plain collarless shirt with a brass stud at the front.

On Sunday my mother and the women of the parish had no opportunity to display their finery. They all wore shawls which, as the saying goes, covered a multitude. Only one lady, the schoolteacher, referred to as Mrs O, wore a hat and coat going into Barraduv Mass. The women's shawls, like the Kinsale cloak, lasted a lifetime. Pride of place went to the paisley shawl of two shades of fawn with a variegated pattern around the base and an abundance of tassels. There was a plain brown shawl, a green and black shawl and a black shawl which widows wore. From a distance a group of women in paisley shawls, their skirts sweeping the ground and with their heads together talking after Mass, looked like a cock of hay. The women always covered their heads with the shawl in the chapel, and a woman in the street who threw the shawl back on her shoulders, twirling the ends of it around her hands and with her arms akimbo while she talked and laughed, was a very outgoing person, something seldom seen.

My mother bought her shawl maybe when she was getting married and the only time she visited the shops was to buy a pair of high buttoned boots and clothes-making materials. Her skirt and blouse, a jacket she called it, she made herself. She made all my clothes as well. She bought the Eton collar, bow tie and of course my boots, but the jacket and trousers she made often from an old suit of my father's turned inside out. She knitted my stockings and my father's and when we put our toes or heels through them they were darned. Cardigans and jumpers she knitted for the household. My jacket, shirt and trousers were sewn by hand. Very few had sewing machines. The traveller, Mr Roycroft, called to the house in his gig trap but we never had enough money to buy one.

I wore a real suit made by Con the tailor for my first holy communion. He fitted me out with a nice body coat and a short pants in which I looked well with a collar and tie like the men and a navy skullcap with yellow stripes.

I dreaded the day before holy communion when I had to go to confession for the first time. The teacher acted it all out for us in school. The examination of our conscience, the going in the door of the confessional when our turn came, making sure to close it after us, waiting for the slide to come across and then saying, 'Bless me father, for I have sinned!' I could hardly go to sleep at night worrying about the sins I would have to tell the priest. I was afraid of what he would say if I had sins to tell and I was afraid of what he would say if I hadn't. I would have to get it right and I knew it was a sin to make a bad confession. 'I didn't do what I was told, father.' This was an example of a sin which the teacher told us. Her version of it was, 'I was disobedient, father'. Maybe it was a sin to make up a sin for the sake of having something to tell. 'I stole sugar, father,' and 'I cursed and swore,' were the other sins I could confess. I made up my mind before I went to sleep the night before that my last sin to tell him would be, 'I told lies, father.' The lies I told were harmless but it gave me something to say.

When the time came the biggest fright I got was the darkness in the penitent's side of the confessional when I closed the door. I wanted to dash out again, but when the slide came across a little light came in, and by rising off my knees I could see the priest inside. He never looked at me and didn't seem a bit surprised when I told him it was my first confession. He asked me to tell him my sins and I rattled off about being disobedient, stealing sugar, telling lies and cursing and swearing. It didn't knock a shake out of him. He gave me my penance, which was three Hail Marys and three Glories. Then for the first time he lifted his head and looked at me and whispered very earnestly, 'Pray for me, my child!' I came out of the box with a weight off my mind and thinking that the priest must be in some sort of trouble seeing that he was asking me to pray for him.

The following day was my first holy communion, the most joyous day in all our lives, the priest said, when he visited the school. The day when we would for the first time receive the body of our Blessed Lord into our souls. The teacher had gone over it all with us. The going up to the altar, kneeling, and joining our hands. Opening our mouths and sticking out our tongues, not too far the teacher warned, to receive the sacred host. Then as we walked in line with our hands joined back to our places, we were to give thanks to God for coming into our souls as we swallowed the host. But what would happen if I couldn't swallow it, I thought, as I lay in bed the night before. Would the host melt in my mouth and then the body of our Blessed Lord would evaporate and not go down my throat and into my soul! Supposing I got a fit of coughing. I turned over on the tick and covered my head. Supposing I coughed the host out on the ground. What would happen then? I couldn't pick it up. The host was sacred and we were told that no hand could touch it but the priest's because his hand had been anointed. Everyone would notice me. The priest would be mad vexed at having to come down off the altar and pick the sacred host off the floor. My mother would be mortified and my father would be dying with the shame.

I went to sleep and dreamt that a frog came into the bed and was trying to get into my mouth. His huge protruding eyes frightened me, and he puffed and he puffed and his belly went in and out like a bellows. Then he began to swell into a monster and I woke up shouting, my body in a lather of sweat. I was in bed with my two younger brothers and my mother, hearing me shout, got up and lit a candle. She put me sitting at the side of the bed and noticing that my body was wet with sweat she dried me and put on a clean shirt.

'You'll be all right now, *a stór*. I'll give you a cup of hot milk.' My mother's cure for everything.

'You can't do that!' my father reminded her. 'The child is fasting.'

From twelve o'clock the night before no bite or sup went inside the lips of a person going to holy communion. A neighbour used to eat at half past twelve, claiming that from where we lived there was a difference of half an hour between Greenwich and God's time, which was the time he went by. I went to sleep again and was up early next morning. There was a lot of fussing over me. My boots were polished and polished again. I had trouble putting a knot in my necktie. My father had to do it for me and my mother said that he made the knot too clumsy and she re-knotted it. Had I a handkerchief? On Sunday mornings there was a clean handkerchief for everyone from the pile of ironed laundry my mother had done the night before.

We had a tub trap for the pony by this time and very well she looked under it in a shiny set of harness. A shake of holy water before we set out to keep us safe on our journey. We all sat in. A rope rein guided Fanny the mare when she was tackled to the common car, but in the trap my father held a leather reins. He sat at the back with my mother and we youngsters at the front. I loved the motion of the trap when we were on level ground and Fanny could trot. Slow-moving asses and carts we passed and fast-moving horses and sidecars passed us. Neighbours waved to me, seeing me in my new rig-out, acknowledging that it was a big day for me.

We didn't have a family pew in the church. They were for the well-to-do farmers, shopkeepers and teachers, who could afford to buy a new pew and pay the yearly rent for it. Some of those seats were never full, yet outsiders never sat in them and I don't think they would be welcome. The family pew was private property in a public place. One year the parish priest put up the rental and a family, thinking the charge was dear enough, refused to pay. The parish priest ordered them out of the seat. They refused and the priest had the pew taken out and put behind the church, where in the end it rotted. The family never went to Mass in that church again during that parish priest's reign, but drove all the way to the friary in town. They never spoke to the parish priest after. Even when he came to the stations in their house they didn't speak, because they felt he had humiliated them before their neighbours and friends. There was a large space behind the seats and those of little property or none stood or knelt there, the men at the gospel side and the women at the side of the epistle. It was strange that among the poor there was segregation, while in the pews husbands sat with their wives.

I knelt with my father. He knelt on one knee, under which he had his cap. My mother, who was across the aisle, frowned when she saw me kneeling on my new skullcap. There was an understanding that the children for first holy communion would go to the altar first and when the time came I got the beck from my mother and I joined the other children as we moved towards the altar. Heads bowed, our hands joined, tips of fingers under the chin, and I with my skullcap under my left oxter. As I moved along I kept repeating the prayer before communion and reminding myself that when I had said the prayer after communion I should pray for my father and mother and all the family. I knelt at the rail, putting my hands under the long white cloth and holding it under my chin and I could hear the priest pray as he came from the far end. An altar boy accompanying him held a little silver tray under the ciborium as the priest laid the host on the communicant's tongue. *O Dia linn*! God be with us! The priest was at the next child to me and the altar boy was placing the silver tray under my chin. 'Corpus Christi,' the priest said and I opened my mouth and put my tongue out. I hoped my tongue would look clean. I washed it in the morning, making sure not to swallow a drop of the water. The priest placed the white circular host on my tongue and I felt the backs of his fingers touch my lips. I closed my mouth and forgot to get up so the boy beside me had to give me a nudge. As I walked back to my place, full of strange feelings of having God in my mouth, I swallowed and nothing happened. Sweet and Blessed Lord, what was wrong? I felt with the tip of my tongue and found that the sacred host had clung to the roof of my mouth. I tried to dislodge it and I couldn't. Terror seized me as I knelt by my father's side. I thought that God was refusing to go into my soul. Did I make a bad confession? Had I done something that offended Him?

'Are you all right, *a leanbh* (my child)?' my father said.

I nodded. I was afraid to open my mouth in case the host fell out. A corner of the host seemed to lift from my palate. I manoeuvred it on to my tongue and with a quick swallow it was gone. I could breath freely now. I looked up. My mother had been watching me. She smiled.

I was starving after the long fast as I came out of the chapel with my father. All the men put on their hats and caps and felt in their coat pockets for their pipes. These were lit and smoke began to rise as we came through the chapel gate. The men didn't make much wonder of me. One man said to my father, 'Is this Brian?' thinking that I was called after my grandfather. My mother came out with her friends. They all admired me in my new clothes. Relations gave me money, small coins, but I got a half-crown from my godmother, Bridgie Lar. I went then to Danny O's shop where my mother bought the messages. Danny O's sister Nora gave me a cup of tea and a currant bun. I took a bite of the bun and a slug of the tea and I was in heaven. We trotted home. Fanny the mare seemed in a hurry. She was hungry and I was too, despite the bun and the tea. A neighbour had killed a pig two days before and last night the gift plate had come to our house. 'Bring in a few kippens (sticks),' my mother said. We did and the fire lit up and in no time the kettle was boiling and a circle of black pudding was sizzling in the pan.

VII

FORBIDDEN FRUIT

Not long after receiving my first holy communion I came
home from school one evening to be told by my mother that
she had met her distant cousin in town that day. Her cousin
was Miss O, a teacher at Lissivigeen School, about the same
distance in the other direction from our house as the school
we attended. Miss O was teaching infants, first and second
class and she asked my mother to let her two boys come to
her school. My father was opposed to the change but my
mother got her way and one Tuesday morning my brother
Tim and I set out for our new school at Lissivigeen. We didn't
start on Monday because there was a superstition about
beginning anything on Monday. My neighbours began no
enterprise on Monday. If a burial was on that day the first
sod of the grave was dug on Sunday. Our hair was never cut
on Monday and the clippings were not put in the fire, but
carefully placed in a hole in the ditch until we came back for
them on the day of the resurrection.

Through some misunderstanding, my brother and I were
put in the same class. He was better than me at many
subjects, which proved an embarrassment to me for the rest
of my schooldays. Miss O was exceptionally nice to us at first,

although we could see how strict she was with the others. One of her punishments for mistakes was holding a pencil between the first and second fingers of her closed fist with a little of the pencil protruding and hitting you hard on the top of the head. This was extremely painful, as I found out when I failed to answer a question which was easily answered by my brother. For grave offences like being late for school, offending pupils were sent up to the master to be slapped.

The master was at the other side of the glass partition and had charge of third, fourth, fifth and sixth classes. He had an ashplant fairly thin so that it almost swung around your hand when he hit you. The sting of the pain went to the heart and there was always a slap on each hand. It was a very hard case who didn't cry, and as they cried the pupils blew into their hands in an effort to ease the pain or pressed their palms under their armpits.

I was fortunate in escaping most of this punishment and my brother was so good that he was never reprimanded. If we were late in the morning I was blamed because I was older and always took the rap. We left home early enough but when we met up with the other scholars on the way we dallied, talked, argued, even sat by the roadside and watched the farmers working in the fields. A horse-drawn mowing machine because of the noise it made we found fascinating. Losing all sense of time, we spun castle tops, and then, of a sudden, realising the lateness of the hour, we plucked a yellow birdsfoot trefoil flower which grew by the roadside. We called it 'no blame' and put it in our books, hoping it would save us from the rod. But it never did.

Only once do I remember being severely slapped and that was when I went with some other boys to rob Owen Keeffe's orchard at play hour. Between getting there and stealing the apples and eating them the time flew and we were very late getting back to school after the bell went. Our hearts sank when we saw that there were no pupils in the playground. We heard the voices in the classrooms reading aloud or doing their tables. For a moment we thought of running away but we had to go in — our satchels were inside. Very timidly and in hangdog fashion we sloped into Miss O's classroom. We were late, we told her, because we had gone to Healy's shop for tobacco for our fathers. Where was the tobacco? We had nothing to show but the telltale apples left over after the feast.

We shook at the knees as she ushered us into the master and told him what we had done. He talked about the seventh commandment and he got the pupils who were preparing for confirmation to recite for us what was forbidden by that commandment, 'unjustly taking what belongs to another . . .' He took the ashplant, looped it almost double and let it go with a swish. He told us to empty our pockets of the few apples we had left, and they were placed on his rostrum. He motioned us then to stand by the wall. Anticipating the pain of punishment as we stood under the map of the world was very near unbearable. When the time for class change came, we were called out one by one. It was better to be first because you didn't know what was coming. What did come was four slaps, two on each hand. The second slap on an aching palm was the hardest to bear and we went back to Miss O's classroom contrite and tearful. When she wasn't looking, my brother, who didn't go on the raid, asked me if I had any apples left. The punishment changed my attitude to robbing orchards for a long time to come. Later when the boys went on another raid, after school this time, I refused to go, remembering the sting of pain from the ashplant which went through my system like an electric shock.

Ashman was what the pupils nicknamed the master,

because of his dexterity with the rod. But to be fair to him he didn't slap all that often. After I moved from Miss O's section into third class I don't think I was ever slapped again. When things went well and everybody did his best and attended to his homework, life in class was great. The master was kindly and had all our interests at heart. There was a lesson once a week to which we all looked forward. This was the hour we spent in the garden attached to the school residence. The big boys dug with spades in the spring and made drills for potatoes and ridges for onions. We were shown how to grow carrots, parsnips, lettuce, and one year we grew a giant vegetable marrow. Currant and gooseberry trees were added to the garden and there was much celebration among the boys the spring we planted four apple trees, winks and nudges, as much as to say we won't have far to go when these bear fruit. In the autumn we harvested the fruits of our labour. Peas and beans were spread out to dry on the wide sills of the school windows, the ripe onions filling the classroom with their pungent smell.

It took the apple trees in the school garden ages to bear fruit, and then one spring there were blossoms on a tree. Not a great number but we watched with the master as a honey bee perched on a flower and, poking for the honey, brought away on its hairy legs the yellow dust which pollinated the next flower. We watched too as the blossoms faded and in time a nut-like little apple appeared. In September there were four apples on the tree. We raced ahead of the master on each weekly visit to see how they were progressing. Coming to the end of the month the apples got larger and the master was very proud of his crop but there was many a young stalwart whose teeth swam in his mouth for a bite of one of the apples. There being only four one would easily be missed if stolen. But a greedy descendant of Adam tasted the forbidden fruit without plucking the apple. He took a large bite from the side away from the public gaze so that it was some days before the master noticed. There was an inquiry, the rod lying waiting on the rostrum, and even though we suspected who the culprit was he was never brought to book. The incident was forgotten and we continued to enjoy the hour we spent each week away from lessons in the garden, out in the open air, preparing the soil, planting the tiny seeds and waiting for them to show above the ground and grow to maturity. It brought us more satisfaction than we got from reading, writing and arithmetic.

When it came to geography, in our first year with the master, he got us to draw a map of the place where we lived showing the house and the fields around it. My map was small, one field, but that was divided into the potato garden, onion and cabbage patch and pasture for the cow and the pony. We were to add in as an extension of our own map the main road, byroads, streams, rivers and any landmarks. There was a *gallán* stone standing on a hillock like a mighty grave not far from our house. We suspected that under the great mound of earth and with the *gallán* stone to mark his resting place, a king or giant of old was taking his long last sleep. The road to school and beyond it to the town we drew, and showed the course of the river Flesk as it wound its way to the lakes of Killarney. We put in the range of mountains which stood on guard over our territory and named them from the Paps to the MacGillicuddy Reeks. If we craned our necks in the schoolyard we could see Carrauntoohil, the highest peak. From our home-made map the master took us to the map on the wall where we learned about Kerry, then about Ireland and a little about the globe. Having started at home and learned about our own surroundings gave us a better understanding of the wider world.

Mangerton Mountain we could see by standing up in the classroom. Mangerton was volcanic maybe a million years ago, the master told us. The crater can still be seen up at the top. It is now a bottomless lake known as the Devil's Punch Bowl. The master laughed as he told us the tall story, often related by the jarveys and boatmen to the tourists, about the man who fell into the Punch Bowl and came out in Australia. Later in a higher class when we came to study *Mo Scéal Féin* (*My Story*) by an tAthair Peadar Ó Laoghaire, we read of a description of a visit to the top of Mangerton which the priest had undertaken as a young student. From up there he could see north to the Shannon, east to Tipperary, south to Bantry Bay and west to the mighty Atlantic pounding on the coast of Kerry. The master was full of admiration for the young student who set out on that trip and we marvelled at the wonders he saw.

Going home that evening we sat on a mossy bank and looking up at the great mountain we said to ourselves why shouldn't we climb it. The idea took root and there and then we made up our minds that we would climb it tomorrow. We would meet at Mac's arch and go over Gortacoosh and up by the shores of Lough Guitane to the foot of Mangerton. We were not sure if we should tell our parents. Maybe we should say that we were going playing football. I went to bed early that night and spent a long time awake, thinking of what I would see from the top of Mangerton. What would our house look like from away up there? Maybe I would not be able to see it with all the trees and bushes that were growing up around the place. I went to sleep at last and dreamt that I was walking like a mighty man and stepping from Mangerton to Ceapach, then to Crohane and Stoompa and finally standing with a foot on each of the twin Paps Mountains. From that position I bent down and washed my face in

Doocorrig Lake. It was the sound of the water trickling through my giant fingers and falling into the lake that woke me up. I listened in the darkness and heard the rainwater gurgling from the eaves into the downpipe and the raindrops falling on the roof.

It rained all the next day and the day after. In time, other things happened to claim our attention.

Two Christian Brothers came to the school one day and talked about their order, their work in foreign lands and the importance of devoting one's life to God. They made the life of holiness, teaching, caring for the sick and travelling abroad very appealing and asked us to join the order. So as not to disappoint the master, who was a very religious man, I was tempted to join up. When they asked us again and with more fervour this time, I was carried away and put up my hand. The master with a smile on his face and a whisper of 'good man' wrote my name and address and gave it to one of the brothers. He took me out into the hallway and asked me all about myself. My age. Was I a good scholar at school? Did I like games? Did I go to the sacraments regularly and what did my father do? He put his hand on my head and said, 'Give yourself to God!'

Then I thought of what my father would say. I had been helping him in the workshop and he often said he was waiting for the time when I would be confirmed and leave school to become his apprentice. He deserved my help as much as God and the black people of Rhodesia. I kept to myself on the way home from school. I didn't know whether the boys thought me very brave or a right ould cod for doing what I did. One boy took out his handkerchief and folded it into a narrow band and put it around his neck to look like a Roman collar. 'Forgive me, Father, for I have sinned!' he mocked. I was encouraged when his comrades said, 'Stop that, Johneen!'

When I reached home I didn't go into the workshop, which was the first thing I always did. Instead I went into the kitchen and told my mother that I was joining the Brothers. In a way she was sort of pleased about it and was full of questions about where I was going, what the Brothers were like and what the Brother said who questioned me in the hall. 'I must pray,' she said, 'and we must all pray and ask if your decision is the right one and if God wants you.'

We went out together to the workshop and she told my father. He was furious. I'll never forget the look he gave me. He threw a tantrum. He kicked things around in his anger. My mother was consoling him and saying what good I'd be doing in the world. 'He'll be praying for you, Ned!' she told my father. 'He'll be praying for you and praying for all of us.' 'Praying won't bore holes in oak, ma'am,' he thundered, as he sank the axe in the chopping block and rived it in two. At the rosary that night I never mentioned a word to God about being a Christian Brother and my mother never asked Him to enlighten me in my decision. She knew if she brought up the subject even at prayers my father would get up off his knees and go out and commune with the stars, something which he did to avoid fighting with my mother in front of us. Some time later a letter came from the monastery saying that I was accepted as a postulant in the order. My mother showed it to me, but by now my mind had changed. 'I think I'll be a carpenter,' I told her. She wrote back to say that I had no vocation.

The Gaelic League in Killarney proposed holding a feis in the old cricket field. Now that the English had gone, men in whites no longer played there. The feis, or festival, celebrating the Irish language, was held in the month of June. We went in the pony and trap. The master had made up a conversation piece in Irish, a *comhrá beirte*, for my brother and myself. We were to act the parts of two old farmers selling a pretend cow at a fair. As well as the *combrá beirte* section there were short plays and sketches, school choirs, storytelling for adults and schoolchildren, stepdancing and solo traditional singing for young and old. Platforms were erected here and there throughout the field so that the audience moved about from competition to competition. Lorries were driven in and with one side butt left down they took the place of platforms.

I was interested in seeing boys and girls of my own age in school plays. One of these was being acted out on the back of a lorry. Pieces of cardboard had fireplaces, doors and windows drawn on them with coloured chalk and placed on the lorry to give the effect of a kitchen scene with the barest essentials in furniture. The first child to enter the stage set stood inside the door and talked back to the one coming in after him. They stood there arguing their case. As each extra actor entered they moved a little bit to make room and the entire play went ahead as they stood in a bunch inside the door. Fireplace, window, chairs and table were all ignored. The man of the roads character wore a white wig and a red beard. His back was bent; he was a martyr to rheumatism. A girl played the grandfather and a boy his wife. They were dressed suitably for the parts but this did not conceal their gender. Their teacher sat on the hood of the lorry prompting them and was overcome with paroxysms of laughter at every funny thing they said. The pupils must have come from an Irish-speaking district for their language was clear and beautifully spoken and because of that the judges had no hesitation in giving them full marks.

My brother and I did fairly well with our *combrá beirte* but spent too much time trying to control an imaginary, recalcitrant cow and lost marks. There was a section for music and this and the school choirs drew the biggest audience. There was an interest too in the child storytellers and a greater interest in the adult exponents of the art. One old man told the story of *Bithiúnach Mór Gleann Fleisce* (The Great Rogue of Glenflesk) and those who could follow what he was saying knocked a tremendous kick out of it because Glenflesk was our parish. The Glenflesk rogue had a school for training young rogues and the storyteller said that many of these students emigrated afterwards and wound up as the biggest gangsters in America.

The official opening was not at the outset of the feis but well into the proceedings, when a full crowd had assembled. It wouldn't do to have a prominent person giving the *óráid na feise* (feis oration) to the few people who would arrive on time. The man who opened our feis was a *duine mór le rá*, a very important person, one of the foremost politicians of the day. There was a great surge forward when he appeared on the platform, such was the esteem in which he was held by most of the people. He spoke only in Irish in a dreary, matter-of-fact tone. The day was very hot and as he went on and on the older women, who had rushed to the fore because of their admiration for him, were now melting with the heat in the tightly packed crowd. They were easing their heavy shawls back on their shoulders to get some air. At first among themselves they had been full of praise for the speaker and mentioned in tones of adulation that it wasn't Irish alone he could speak but French and German. The great man droned on and as the women were being overcome with the heat and unable to get out and not understanding one word of what he said their interest waned. One old lady, shifting from foot to foot, the sweat running down her face and glistening in the little hollow below her throat, remarked in a voice of pure desperation, 'Oh God, will he ever stop the *cadarál*ing!' She knew at least one word in Irish, which meant meaningless meandering. Suddenly the oration was at an end; the people parted, letting the air circulate, and the women, feeling cooler, went off to get themselves some refreshment. The same as at the City or a sports meeting, there was lemonade for sale. This on a hot day was in great demand, as were the fat biscuits which went with it.

In one part of the field there was a tug-of-war between schools to give those not too proficient in the language a chance to show their talents. There was high jumping too and a bag race and spoon race. I was on the tug-of-war team from our school and so was Paddy Furnane. Paddy had his head down and with his heel he was making an impression in the ground that he could dig into while straining on the rope. Two priests, one with an umbrella – some priests carried umbrellas at all times – were walking along deeply engaged in conversation and not watching where they were going. One of them thrust his patent leathered foot under Paddy's heel as it was coming down and got the full force of the steel tip on his toe cap. The priest growled with pain and lifted the injured foot, hopping on the other one. He was red-haired, a sign of temper, and seeing Paddy and associating him with his agony he upped with the umbrella and landed Paddy the father and mother of an ecclesiastical clout on top of the head and floored him. Paddy got up, staggered around holding his head and then made a beeline for the gate of the cricket field, leaving us to pull the tug-of-war without him. We were beaten badly. The proceedings were closed by a pipers' band playing for a while and then marching out the gate. We all followed them.

VIII

A Strong and Perfect Christian

The one time while I was at the master's side of the partition when he became very angry was when we were studying for confirmation. The religious doctrine we had to learn was much harder than that for holy communion. Reams of the catechism had to be got off by heart. Our not too supple tongues had to get around words like consanguinity. 'Big rocks of words,' our elders used to say, 'that you wouldn't break in a County Council stone crusher!'

Q What else is forbidden by the sixth commandment?
A All lascivious looks and touches, idleness and bad company; all excesses of eating and drinking and whatever may tend to inflame the passions.

God help us! All we ever saw in flames was a furze bush! My mother held the book for me and listened to my answers, and was as liable to lose her temper as the master if I got them wrong. I didn't mind her getting mad with me and anyway she didn't slap as the master did. There was no explanation from the master or my mother as to what the words we didn't understand meant. I had only to guess what

77

was implied by, 'Thou shalt not covet thy neighbour's wife.'

The men had a story in our rambling house when they heard me mention that commandment. It seems a young lad who had been away for a long time with his uncle in County Limerick missed out on the sacrament of confirmation. When the lack was discovered he was almost twenty and even though of a wild and obstreperous nature he was sent back to school where he sat with boys nearly half his age learning his catechism. On the appointed day the bishop came to the church to confirm the children. He walked down the aisle not yet in his full canonicals and questioned a class as they sat, school by school, in the body of the church. The bishop couldn't help noticing a grown man sitting in the middle of the children and he consulted with the parish priest who was at his side. In whispered tones he was told of the circumstances. The bishop commenced to question the young man and he gave a good enough account of himself until he was asked what was forbidden by the ninth commandment. 'Thou shalt not converse with thy neighbour's wife,' he said. The bishop smiled and gave the correct answer. And then in an effort to make the meaning plain he said, 'Would it be correct for you to fall in love with your neighbour's wife?' 'Why should I do a thing like that, my lord,' the young man said, 'and the country full of young lovely girls!'

Well, our day came to go under the bishop's hand. The priest came to the school, examined us and gave each one of us a ticket. We were seated school by school in the lofty cathedral, the teacher responsible for the tuition standing or kneeling with each group. Surpliced priests walked among us asking questions here and there. Then the bishop came out of the sacristy followed by two young priests. They remained behind the altar rails, one of them holding the bishop's mitre and the other his crozier. The bishop had a surplice over a red soutane and a big cross on a gold chain hung from his neck. When he came nearer we saw the huge ring with a red diamond bulging from it on his right hand; the sign, we were told, of his authority. The bishop paused and asked a few questions of a school and if the answering was good he passed on to the next class. But when he came to a school where the answering was indifferent he stayed and questioned them thoroughly and then spoke to the parish priest, as if voicing his disappointment at the quality of the religious instruction. Small as we were, we had pity for that school's master standing there as red as a turkeycock.

I thought the bishop was going to pass by our school but no, he paused and looked straight at me. I began to shake, I was so nervous. He asked a question but it was the boy beside me who answered it. He moved on. The question was about perjury. Perjury was a reserved sin in our diocese. Maybe that was why I got tongue-tied. A while earlier I had been before the court as a witness in a lawsuit between two neighbours over a right of way. One party had erected a gate in the passageway to which the other party objected. I used to help drive the objector's cattle and said in court that the gate was always closed against us, which wasn't exactly true. There were a few, very few times when it was open, but I didn't tell the court that because it would weaken my party's case. I would have been as well off telling the truth because we lost the lawsuit and the gate is still there.

How well now the bishop wanted to ask me about perjury. My heart missed a beat. I hadn't confessed that transgression and I was going to receive the sacrament of confirmation with my soul in a state of sin. A small consolation came to comfort me. I remembered the judge had said that day in court that I was too young to be sworn in. 'Where will you go, my boy,' the judge asked me, 'if you tell a lie?' 'To hell, my lord,' I told him. I was becoming easier in my mind now because I couldn't have committed perjury if I wasn't sworn in. It was just a lie. Bad enough, God knows, but I would make an act of contrition with a firm purpose to sum up enough courage to tell the priest about it the next time I went to confession. I said an act of contrition then and I put my whole heart into it.

The candles were lit on the altar, the choir sang and the priests helped the bishop to finish his vesting. The mitre was given to him, he took it in both hands, looked into it and put it on his head. Then he put his hand round to make sure that the two broad ribbons that fell from the mitre hadn't gone down inside his chasuble. He took the crozier in his left hand, drew himself up rooster-like to his full height and stood as still as eternity for a moment in all his finery; it was an impressive sight. If I ever became a priest I'd want to end up as a bishop.

We went to the altar rails school by school and knelt down. Almost everyone had new clothes. My suit was navy blue and made by Con the tailor. The bishop approached along the line, preceded by a priest holding a vessel with holy oils or chrism into which the bishop dipped the thumb of his right hand. He made the Sign of the Cross on my forehead. Holding his hand over me he pronounced the words of the sacrament and gave me a light slap with his open palm on the cheek. I looked up at him and he eyed me back. I didn't flinch. My mother always told me to look the world in the eye. 'Make no excuses for yourself,' she said. 'You are as good as anyone else.' Words which echoed what the master made us learn by heart from Ó Cadhlaigh's 'Slighe an Eolais' (The way of knowledge):

THE APPRENTICE

Is gael mise agus mise im Ghael,
Ni thuigim gur náir dom é
Ni chasfainn mo chúl le fearaibh an tsaoil;
Is ní fearr d'fhear cach ná mé.

(I am Irish and Irish I am,
Of that I am not ashamed.
I would not turn my back
To the men of the world,
And there is no man
Better than I am!)

Walking back to my place I thought to myself not alone was I as good as the next but after confirmation I was a strong and perfect Christian, provided of course that God accepted the act of contrition in place of my bad confession. God is good, I always heard, and he has a good mother. I prayed to her now as my own mother had told me do and asked her to intercede for me with her divine son, and for all the family.

Now that I was confirmed I knew that my days at school were numbered. I'd leave when I was fourteen and follow the trade of my father and grandfather. Already during the school holidays I was helping my father in the workshop, keeping a car shaft steady while he was mortising it for the cross laths or turning the handle of the grindstone. I tried my hand at planing and sawing or drilling deep holes in wood with the auger or bit and brace. At night on the kitchen table I'd rewrite, so that we'd have a copy, the long list of materials down to the last nail, when my father was engaged to do the carpentry work of a new house. Masons built the house in stonework and my father made the doors and windows, staircase and partitions. He put on the roof and slated it and put down the timber floors. Away from school in the summertime I loved getting on the roof and helping to nail the slate laths to the rafters. Nothing gave me more pleasure than clouting two-inch wire nails into timber. When the last lath was on, I'd walk on the inch-and-a-quarter ridge board, with my hands out like an acrobat on a tightrope from chimney stack to chimney stack. My father would nearly have a heart attack watching me but he wouldn't shout in case I'd fall.

In a short time my father was allowing me to cut the 'bird's mouth' on the heel of a rafter where it fits over the wall plate, or letting me chisel out the chase in the string boards of the staircase to receive the step and the riser. The rough preliminary work I would do like Michelangelo's apprentice and my father would finish it himself. He had the name of being a great man at his trade and it was a joy to watch him working and a pleasure to see him when a job was finished, the staircase for instance, complete with balusters, handrail, newel post and bull-nosed step, and the way he would stand back from it, his head a little to one side, admiring his handiwork. I looked forward to the time when school would be over and I could be with him every day.

The master's father, a stately old man with a King Edward beard, lived in the school residence. Now and again he came to the school and looked us over with a practised eye, picking out the boys with the brains. He had a tub trap highly polished, and with yellow stripes on the shafts and on the spokes of the wheels. This classy contraption was drawn not by a high stepping horse or pony but by a jennet, a stubborn and cantankerous animal who'd kick the stars and often left the marks of his hind hooves on the under carriage of the trap. One morning on our way to school we met the master's father in the trap. As he passed us he lifted the whip crop and said, 'Good morning, boys!' To which we all answered, 'Good morning, Master!' The jennet must have taken exception to this greeting and as the gate of Mick Horgan's field was open the jennet suddenly wheeled across the road, almost knocking us down and dashed into the field. The old man stood up in the trap and, tugging at the reins, tried to bring him to a halt but it was no good. The jennet galloped three rounds of the field, making a strange neighing sound, with his tail stuck above the front board of the trap. Then he ran out the gate again and continued on his journey. We would have cheered that morning at what looked like a one-jennet chariot race but we knew the story would go back to our own master and we'd never hear the end of it.

Sometimes when the master's father came to the school he would say to his son. 'I want two boys to come to the house and clean out the jennet's droppings.' We were afraid of the jennet but still if picked out we would go gladly because it could kill maybe an hour away from lessons. One day I was selected with a boy from Ballaugh. We plodded after the old man over to the house. He showed us the shed where the jennet was stabled and gave us a fork and coarse brush to clean out from him. We thought it strange that he didn't take the jennet out of the shed while we were cleaning it. Maybe he forgot. We opened the door of the shed and went in. The jennet was tied with a rope running from a halter to a ring in the wall beside his manger. When he saw us he bared his teeth and put both his ears lying along his neck, a sure sign that he had evil on his mind. He threw a few kicks in our direction and collected himself up near the manger. We availed of this opportunity to clean and brush the droppings on to the dunghill outside. We put in fresh straw, going as close to him as we dared. As we made for the door he let fly with the hind hooves. Mercy of God that he didn't brain us. We told the old man that the job was done. He came and looked and was satisfied and gave us sixpence each. When we came back to class the master asked us how we had got on and the boy from Ballaugh, hoping that the master might be talkative, as he sometimes was, asked him why jennets were so cross. The master thought it had to do with their not being a definite species. He took off his glasses and began to polish the lens with his handkerchief, a sure sign that he might spend some time on the subject.

The jennet was a crossbreed, he said, and so was the mule. In the case of the jennet the mother was a horse and the father was a donkey, and it was the other way around for the mule. He paused for a moment as if he wasn't too sure of that statement. These hybrids, he explained, did not breed again, which was just as well as there were enough strange looking animals in the world. They were very rough, stubborn, bad tempered creatures, but were great workers and lived longer than either of their parents. The jennet and mule were in great demand during the Boer War for pulling small cannons over rough ground and when they became scarce large donkeys were used for the same purpose. Then with a half-smile as he warmed to his subject he told us that it was announced in the British House of Commons that an army representative was coming to Ireland to buy as many large donkeys as he could find. Our local MP, seeing an opportunity for farmers to make money, asked that the representative come to Kerry. Spanish donkeys were rounded up in readiness for the sale but the army man never turned up. Very disappointed, the MP asked in the Commons why he hadn't come, to be told that he got his full needs of large donkeys in the midlands and Connemara. 'He made a mistake,' the MP said, 'he should have come south for the biggest asses in Ireland are in Kerry!' We all laughed, ending in a hee-haw. The master looked at us for a while and then, getting serious, said, 'Maybe that MP was right!'

IX

THE REAPER COMES

'Go for the priest!' was the shout we heard from Daniel's high field, the same field where we were saving hay when the British soldiers drove up and down Bohar Vass singing and cheering on the day of the Truce in 1921. Daniel had been working at the hay when he had a seizure. Immediately his son was on his bicycle to the presbytery and someone else went to town for Dr O'Donoghue. Neighbours arrived quickly and one man recited an act of contrition into Daniel's ear as he lay on his back on the ground. His family, the blood drained from their cheeks, were a pitiful sight to see. His wife, her arms around him, cried, 'Don't go! Don't go from us!' As we waited for the priest – and it seemed ages before he came – everything was done to make the sick man comfortable. The neckband of his shirt was loosened and someone brought a bolster from the house to put it under his head. The priest came in long strides across the field. We all moved back as he knelt beside Daniel, feeling for the pulse in his left wrist. With a grim face he took the penitential stole from his pocket, put it about his neck and pronounced the words of absolution. Then he anointed his eyes, lips, ears and we had to take off Daniel's boots and socks so that the last oil could be put on his feet. The young doctor came in over the fence, running from his car. He knew immediately what everyone suspected: that Daniel was dead. The family wept bitterly. His wife, cradling his head on her lap, raised her eyes to heaven and asked God why he had done this to them.

The kitchen door was taken off the hinges and the body placed on it and taken by able-bodied men and placed on his bed. Older women who had done this job before came and washed the corpse. With his own razor he was shaved and, dressed only in his long shirt, he was put lying on the white sheet of the bed. White sheets were draped over the head and foot of the bed. Two blessed candles were lit, one at each side of a crucifix. The clock was stopped and a cloth hung over the only mirror in the room. Later, when supplies for catering at the wake were brought from town, there was a brown friar-like habit which was put on the corpse. Two pennies were put on his eyelids and a prayerbook under his chin. These would be taken away when rigor mortis had set in and the face with the eyes and the mouth shut would look serene. The hands were joined and a rosary beads entwined around the fingers. The white cord was tied around his waist and his grey socks that his wife had knitted for him were put on his feet.

The wake was about to begin. People were already coming in. Women of settled years, near neighbours and relatives of the family by blood or marriage, sat in the wake room with the widow. Men took off their caps coming into the room, knelt by the bedside and said a prayer. Then they sympathised with the widow or any of the family in the room and spoke a few words in praise of the man who was gone. The wife was dry-eyed and composed after hours of weeping, but when a near relative of her own or her husband's came into the room she took them by the hand and cried openly.

Her husband was a great loss, his family not yet reared. The older members had emigrated and were now in America. They wouldn't hear about their father's death until a letter came and then news would spread to his nephews, nieces, cousins and one-time neighbours. They would all come together and there would be another wake three thousand miles away in New York. With the candlelight flickering on the pallid face of the corpse and paler on the faces of the women there was an eerie atmosphere in the wake room. Voices were subdued except when a near relative arrived and cried out on seeing the corpse on the bed. It was heart-warming to see the feeling of love, sympathy and the sense of loss displayed by all who came and the deep respect they showed for the dead.

The kitchen was brighter. There were two oil lamps lighting. Preparations were going ahead for catering for the crowds who would come to the wake, not only tonight but tomorrow night. Neighbouring wives and daughters would see that tea, white shop bread and red jam were provided for all those who came. The provisions brought in the horse cart from town were still being taken into the house. Some families beggared themselves with the amount of money spent on food and drink. Men were tapping a half-tierce of porter and setting it up on a small table in the bottom of the kitchen with a white enamel bucket under the tap. When the last sympathiser had come and everyone was seated, snuff went around in a saucer as the people settled down to wake the corpse. Each person took a pinch of snuff, praying for the soul of the departed. There was much sneezing, which brought choruses of 'God bless us!' or 'God bless you!' In a while's time a man went around with the white enamel bucket full of porter and each man of the older generation got a bowl of the liquid. When they raised the bowl it was not to say, 'Good health!' but 'The light of heaven to his soul!' The women, girls and younger men sat into the table and drank tea and ate bread and jam.

In a corner of the kitchen there were men cutting and crushing tobacco and putting it in clay pipes. Men, again of the older generation and close friends of the man who was gone, were given a pipe, and as they lit the pipes and the smoke curled up, prayers ascended to heaven for their dear friend. The talk among the men and women was about the late owner of this fine house. They spoke about the age he had reached, about his farm and the great warrant he was to work. The men talked about the times they met him at fairs and markets, at wakes and weddings and in the work they did when neighbours came together for threshing oats or cutting turf. They remembered him as a young man at house dances before he married and how when the music struck up he knocked sparks out of the flagged floor. Those feet were now stilled. They looked at the concertina on top of the dresser which his wife played for set dances in this kitchen. That would now be silent. For twelve months his wife and daughters would go to town or church in black mourning, and his sons would wear a black diamond on the left sleeve.

By degrees the talk took on a general tone and as the white bucket went around again the volume of the conversation increased but never so loud that people forgot the sadness which death had brought to their midst that day. In groups men put their heads together the better to hear old men tell stories until before midnight, when it was time to say the rosary. This was started in the wake room and the person who called the mysteries stood in the short passage between the room and the kitchen. After five decades were recited, the Hail, Holy Queen was said and then the litany for the dead began. When God's name was mentioned the response was, 'Have mercy on us!' and when the name of the Virgin or the saints was called the people responded with 'Pray for us!' After the rosary many people went home, but near neighbours and relatives sat and watched and talked and prayed until the grey light came in the window. The next day, relatives who lived far away would come, and that night Daniel would be waked again. On the third morning the funeral would set out for Muckross Abbey.

As the mourners were assembling for the funeral, a tall, stately woman arrived. She was a distant cousin and the first and last person I heard to cry the lament for the dead. At the wicket gate leading to the house she dipped the corner of her apron in her mouth and wet under her eyes to give the appearance of tearstained cheeks. She threw her shawl back on her shoulders and gave a loud cry which sounded like, 'Oh, oh, oh, ochone, oh.' She brought her voice up to a fierce wail, which subsided into a singsong as she walked in the pathway. When she saw the family coming to the door her grief knew no bounds and they all added their voices to hers. Other women joined in as they went through the kitchen to the wake room where the family cried their hearts out. Just as suddenly as it began, there was silence and, as if having shaken off a weight of sorrow, those nearest to the dead man smiled and were contented. I had seen for the last time what had once been the dirge for a dead chieftain, when his genealogy was recited in the old days. It was now only a pale imitation of the ritual it had been then.

The coffin came through the door and was borne on the shoulders of four men of the same surname. Each man wore, as did every male relation, a black crêpe piece on his left coat sleeve. The older men put the length of crêpe around their hats. The crêpe was tied with a black ribbon. A white ribbon was used if the deceased was a young person. The coffin was placed in the horsedrawn hearse. There was a pause then while people got into their transport, and when everyone was ready the hearse moved off, followed by sidecars, then traps and common cars and last in the procession were men on horseback. As we were going through the town, shop doors were shut and in some cases a single shutter put up as a mark of respect. The grave was open when we arrived at Muckross Abbey. Neighbours' sons did the work. Every act connected with the wake and funeral, the catering for the numbers who came to the house, the washing and laying out of the corpse, its placing in the coffin and now the burial, was performed by relatives and friends. All these services were given as a mark of respect for an esteemed neighbour. Death the reaper brought the people together.

The priest read the prayers and sprinkled holy water on the coffin. In the sunlight, drops fell on the breastplate which read, 'Daniel Moynihan, 49 years.' When the coffin was lowered into the grave two men went down and, unscrewing the wing nuts on the lid, placed them in the sign of the cross by the breastplate. This meant something, a nod maybe in the direction of rising on the last day. During the prayers the relatives remained calm. The great cry at the lament that morning seemed to have drained them of their sorrow, but now as the first shovelful of clay fell with a loud noise on the coffin lid they cried out again. Red-eyed and pale-faced, the wife and daughters wept in their black mourning clothes. The lid covered with earth, the noise was reduced to a dull thud and then no noise as the grave was filled and the green sods beaten down with the backs of shovels on the new mound.

The priest led a decade of the rosary and that over, people waited for a while and then drifted away to pray at a family grave before making their way in twos and threes to the graveyard gate. The men and women would go for a drink when they reached the town. Many of the women who didn't like sitting in a pub would crowd into the snug. The man who was gone was the talk of the last three days, and he was talked of again when the men came that night to my father's rambling house, a place where he himself had sat three nights before. They mentioned all the people who came to the dead man's wake and funeral and they all agreed a king couldn't have got a better send-off.

X

The Stations

My mother always wanted to have the stations in our house but it was not to be. The station Mass was said in the farmers' houses. The powers-that-be decided that the occupant of an artisan's dwelling would be unable to meet the expense of catering for a big crowd the morning of the stations. The men around my father's fire did not know the origin of the stations unless they were necessary in the penal times when there were no churches in which to say Mass. They did say that the priests in those days travelled long distances and were put up in the station house the night before. There were at least seven obligations the owner had to meet in connection with the priest's stay: a room, a bed and a fire, food, polish for the priest's boots, oats for his horse and an offering. The men heard tell of the days when the priest was hunted and of the time when there was no presbytery in our parish and only a shack for a church. The parish priest and his curate lived in a one-roomed hovel. The curate was an exceedingly holy man. He'd give the shirt off his back to the poor. One day a beggar asked him for help. The curate told him he had no money, that he had given his last ha'penny to a poor man the evening before. The beggar persisted in his plea for help and asked the curate in the name of the Virgin to give him something. 'Look!' says the curate, turning out his trouser pockets. Half a crown fell on to the road. He gave the money to the beggar and nothing would convince the holy man but that the Blessed Virgin had put the money in his pocket.

At mealtime he told the parish priest about it. 'I am sure and certain,' he said, 'I had no money. It was a miracle!'

'Ah, miracle my hat,' the parish priest replied. 'You'd want to watch whose trousers you are putting on in the morning!'

Twice a year, in the springtime and in the autumn, the station came to our area. There were three small townlands with not many more than a dozen houses in the station district. The station Mass went in rotation and when a man's turn came there was feverish activity in that house to have the place ready for the morning of the big event. The walls were whitewashed inside and out, the roof freshly thatched and the furniture varnished. Varnish put on too late and in a smoky kitchen didn't always dry, and many is the person stuck to the chair he sat on the morning of the stations. Two brothers put their backs to a sticky dresser and when they went to go on their knees before confession, they brought the dresser down on top of them. Such a clatter of broken delf! The parish priest in the room thought it was the end of the world. In the old days we are told, green rushes were cut and spread under the feet of a visiting king, and the muddy approaches to a farmer's door were covered in a similar way under the feet of a priest the morning of the stations.

When the stations came to a neighbour's house my mother would let me and my brother go on before her. I was always there in plenty of time to see the people arrive. The women went straight into the house. Their husbands lingered in the yard in their Sunday suits and polished boots, talking. No pipes — they wouldn't smoke until they had received holy communion. When the parish priest arrived, driven by the parish clerk in a horse and sidecar, the men took off their hats and caps and greeted him. He exchanged a few pleasantries with them and went into the house.

The curate came a little later. He had his own horse and every year a collection was made for the support of the priests' horses. It was called the oats money. After a few words in the kitchen the parish priest went into the parlour where there was a blazing fire, and began to hear confessions. He sat sideways in the chair with his head turned away from the penitent as he heard his sins. The curate heard confessions in the other room, and the parish clerk made the kitchen table into an altar on which to say Mass. The table was raised almost to elbow height by putting two chairs under the cross rails.

The parish clerk had a very large and battered suitcase from which he took the consecrated altar stone and placed it centre-ways and a little to the back of the table. This stone is said to contain a relic. The altar cloth was put over it and let fall down over the sides of the table. The Mass book, two large candlesticks and a chalice were set in their proper places. There were three cards, each with a large ornamented capital letter, from which the priest read during Mass. One was placed at each end and one in the middle with the words of consecration. Over the chalice the clerk put a smaller card and on this was draped a square of cloth of the same material as the priest's vestments. The two sides of the cloth were pulled out at the bottom to give the draped piece the shape of a pyramid without a top, and the letters IHS were at the front.

The parish clerk put a ciborium on the altar and took out a handbell which he put on the floor near him to ring when the chalice and the sacred host were raised at the consec-

ration. I wondered how he fitted everything into that old
suitcase. There seemed to be no end to what it revealed, and
the last things to come out were the priest's vestments. They
were neatly folded and placed at the end of the altar in the
order in which they would go on the priest. I followed the
parish clerk's work with a keen eye and my hands itched to
help him. Most of all the vestments caught my attention and
for a moment I wished I were big enough to put them on.
I tried to remember the different names of the pieces. When
we were studying for confirmation the master had put
pictures of the vestments on the board and told us their
names several times.

The parish priest came from the parlour, leaving whoever
was remaining for confession to go to the curate. In the
crowded kitchen and in the small space in front of the altar
he vested himself. First the amice, a square piece of white
cloth which he wore like a cape; the two strings which hung
from the corners he tied around his middle. He stooped and
the parish clerk put the folded alb over his head, he put his
hands through the sleeves and the long white garment fell to
the floor. He was now handed the cincture, a long white
rope-like cord which he doubled and tied it around his waist,
leaving the tasselled ends fall down his right side. One tassel
almost reached the floor and the other swung a bit above it.
The priest pulled up the alb at the front and back inside the
cincture so that now I could barely see his boots. Next he
put the stole around his neck and crossed it over his breast,
tucking the two ends inside his waistband to keep it in
position. Then he took the maniple, a piece of vestment
material like a short stole, doubled and sewn in such a way
that it ran over his left sleeve and rested between his wrist
and elbow. The last thing to go on was the chasuble, a
sleeveless, open-at-the-sides garment. The parish clerk had

rolled its two sides up and when the priest showed him his stooped head the clerk put the opening down over it and the chasuble rolled down his front and down his back like two maps rolling down a wall.

The parish priest, taking a card from the altar, went on his knees and recited the acts of faith, hope and charity. Now the Mass proper started, answered by the parish clerk, and the Latin sounded strange in the small space of the crowded kitchen. At the consecration the priest whispered fervently the words which we had never heard in the chapel as he rested his elbows on the table and thrust his body back towards us. Soon he would raise the host and as the bell rang every head bowed down as we beat our breasts. In my way of looking at things I thought we bowed down because human eyes could not stand the blinding splendour of God coming on the altar. When I glanced up the chalice was rising in the priest's hands towards the darkness of the interior of the thatched roof, and many women in a voice above a whisper said, 'My Lord and my God!'

The parish clerk had counted the number of people who were to receive holy communion and that number of breads or small hosts had been put in the ciborium to be consecrated.

After the communion the priest put his back to the altar and the kitchen table, so unstable on the chairs, nearly capsized. The priest quickly put his weight back on his feet and the clerk, reaching out, caught the table and saved us all from a calamity. The priest didn't raise his voice as he did in chapel. He gave the sermon in a conversational tone and it was about the truth. 'Thou shalt not bear false witness against thy neighbour.' He was very serious in his condemnation of the liar in everyday life and in the courtroom. Perjury was a reserved sin in our diocese. The priest in confession could not absolve the penitent; he had to go to the bishop. I thought of the day of my confirmation and about the doubts I had, but I had made a good confession since and I wasn't going to worry any more about it. After the sermon the priest turned his back to us and faced the altar and it wasn't long until he came to the last gospel. I followed it in my child's prayer book, 'In the beginning was the word and the word was with God . . .' After the Mass proper there were three Hail Marys and the Hail, Holy Queen.

The priest, getting up from his knees, took off his vestments and gave them to the clerk, who folded them and put them back in the large suitcase. The priest spoke to the men about their work and about the weather. Men considered it an honour to be singled out and spoken to by the priest and a singular honour if he remembered their names. With the table back in its former position, the parish priest sat at the head and the clerk gave him a large account book from which the priest read the names of each householder in the station district. As each name was called out the man or the woman came forward and put the station offering on the table. Seven and six it was. It had gone up since last year. Each three half-crowns as they were put on the table sat there in a little stack, which made one woman remark to the priest, 'You're making hay, Father. Lots of meadowcocks in your field.'

When the dues were collected the parish priest and the curate, who had been talking to the young men in the yard, were invited into the parlour for breakfast. The owner of the house sat with the priests and one or two other men noted for being able to give a good account of themselves. Some parish priests preferred to eat alone, and it was said that one man used to bring his red setter which sat beside him and to which he talked and gave small morsels of food during the meal.

There was much excitement among the women to see

that everything was right. These were the most important guests the woman of the house would ever have in her parlour. If the priest's preference was for boiled eggs the timing of the cooking was vital so that the eggs didn't end up too watery or in bullets. A priest who had been in the parish for a long time, his likes were known, but when a new priest took over the duties of the parish many enquiries were made as to what his preferences in food were. There was always toast: slices of shop bread browned on a long fork in front of the fire.

In the dim and distant past a new priest came and it was said that he liked tea for breakfast. That commodity was unknown in our community then. The woman of the house where the stations were coming was a know-all who had never seen tea in her life but sent to the city for a pound packet of it. She made no inquiries about its preparation but on the morning put the whole lot down in a large saucepan and stewed it well. Then she drained off the liquid, put the tea leaves in a dinner plate and said to the priest, 'Is it a shake of salt or pepper you'll have on it, Father?'

My mother and the other women sitting in the kitchen would give their eyes out for a mouthful of tea. It was a long fast since twelve o'clock the night before, and good enough, when the priests' needs were seen to each woman got a cup in her hand. There would be a full breakfast for everyone when the priests were gone. That was the flurry of excitement when the parish priest got up from the table – getting his horse and the curate's horse. After the goodbyes and when they were well out of sight the bottle of whiskey was produced. With a hint of ceremony the owner tilted the bottle upside down ever so slowly and back again so that the goodness was evenly distributed through the contents. There was more than a tint for all the men of the older generation.

Some savoured the golden liquid, others gulped it down, and there was a drop too for the women if they fancied it. The breakfast was taken in relays. The women took over the priests' place in the parlour and the older men were given the first sitting in the kitchen. There was tea, bread and butter and boiled eggs and red jam for those with a sweet tooth.

If the owner of the house could rise to it there was a bottle of stout for the men and wine for the ladies. Indeed it was not unknown for a man to have a half-tierce of porter, and our ramblers had the story of a house where the barrel of stout was put too near a blazing fire. While the priests were hearing confessions in the rooms the bung flew out of the barrel and a spout of Murphy's stout shot up the chimney. Strong men were quick to the rescue and lifted the half-tierce out the door, one man holding his palm over the bung. They hid it in the cowhouse and nearly wept at the loss of such precious liquid. The kitchen was clean again and everything in its own place when the priest came to say Mass. Even though there was the unmistakable smell of stout he didn't pretend to notice but the theme of his sermon was strong drink.

Friends of the family who couldn't make it to morning Mass called during the day. There was an air of festivity in the townland, a kind of local holiday, and in the house that night there was a station dance. Michael and Brian Kelly brought their concertinas and the room where the consecration bell had rung some hours before now echoed to dancing feet.

XI

AT THE THRESHING

There was always a dance in the houses the night of a threshing. It was a celebration when something was achieved, a kind of thanksgiving like saying thank you to God for visiting the house the morning of the stations. The first threshing machine I saw was in Murphy's haggard, and it was worked by a pair of horses running in a circle and turning a shaft which turned another on which there was a wheel which operated the threshing machine. The next thresher I saw in the same place was worked by a steam engine. It had a funnel like a train engine and when coal was fed into it and it had water in the tank it belched smoke and steam hissed out of various parts of it. There was a huge wheel at the side, which carried a belt attached to the axle of the threshing drum. When in operation it made a loud throbbing noise that could be heard miles away.

The corn ripened around Puck Fair, 11 August, and men with scythes fell in to mow it, cutting the standing stems towards the growing corn. The swathes lay with the ears of grain falling in the same direction. The takers lifted the corn in bundles from the swathe and laid them in rows. Then the binders came and took some stems of corn and twisted them rope fashion and tied each bundle near the base to form a sheaf. My mother was a neat binder. Being a farmer's daughter, she had worked in the fields as a young girl. She would give a day binding to a neighbour and afterwards there would be a present of a sack of potatoes and fresh vegetables for the table. The farmer would let her glean the stray stalks of corn. She brought a huge bundle and shook out the straw for our hens. They enjoyed scratching their way through it and pecking up the grain. The cock was very much to the fore in this operation, and when he found a choice morsel he made a loud clucking noise and with a little side dance called his favourite hen to share it with him. When the hens had pecked the grain we had the straw to use as bedding for the cow and the pony.

A mower in full flight was a pleasure to watch. The rhythmic swing of the scythe and the swish of the blade as it cut through the corn was music to the ear. His feet were spaced about eighteen inches apart and as he never lifted them from the ground his boots left two marks in his wake like the track of a car. The mower worked without coat or waistcoat with his sleeves folded up and his braces hanging down his trouser legs. The good mower was a man who could keep the blade of his scythe sharp. There was a narrow board attached to the scythe which had a coating of carborundum at each side, and after mowing a few swathes the mower placed the tip of the blade on the ground and sharpened the back end of it. He rubbed the board to the two sides of the cutting edge with a quick semi-circular motion making a dit-dit dit-dah sound. Then, holding the blade over his shoulder he sharpened the tip and the sound went dit-dit dit-day.

Towards evening the sheaves of oats were put standing on end and leaning together in the fashion of rifles stacked in a barrack yard. The stooks were placed in neat rows and a few days later, in case of rain, the stooks were capped by putting sheaves around them. Building a load of corn on a horse car to bring it into the haggard was a skilful piece of work. The ends of the sheaves were to the outside and by leaving the wheel guards on the car the square load was built out over the wheels and sloped forward over the horse's back. Two ropes slung over it tied the load down to the car. In the haggard, circles of stones were put down to form the base of the stacks. The stones saved the corn from the damp. The base was covered with rushes or briars and the sheaves of corn built on that. When the circular stack was at a height of about ten feet it looked like a truncated inverted cone widening as it went up. At this stage an eave was formed from which the roof of the stack tapered to a point.

A farmer with a good crop of oats would have four or five stacks in his haggard. Sitting all together they looked like a village of strange houses in some distant land. One stack was thatched with green rushes and sat there for the winter. Sheaves were pulled from it evenly all round so that the stack sank down smaller as time passed. These sheaves were fed to the horses or hand-scutched if straight unbroken straw stems were needed for thatching the farmhouse.

It could be late September before the threshing mill got round to every farm. When the mill was set up in the haggard, neighbouring men came to help feed the sheaves into the drum, and neighbouring girls came to assist at the catering for such a big crowd or to draw the grain to the *síogóg* (straw granary). People of the district came together when a job needed many hands. The system was called comhairing and the labour was returned by the farmer or his servant boy.

The straw granary to hold the grain was what I loved to see being made. A circular stone base was prepared and

covered with old sacking. Then an endless súgán, a straw
rope about six inches thick, was twisted and laid in a circle
on the base. This circling of the rope was continued, making
a circular wall, four feet in diameter at the bottom and
widening out like the haystack as it went up. The grain was
poured into the middle and when it was packed down it kept
the straw rope in place. It reached its required height when
there was no more grain to go in. A wide eave, made with
sheaves, was added, and a conical roof of straw which was
thatched with rushes. The *síogóg* sitting there as the daylight
faded looked like a fairy house with its dark green roof and
golden base. It was flanked by a rick of straw and a rick of
hay. The day's work over, they stood in the now silent
haggard as the moon shone and the sound of music came
faintly from the farmhouse, growing louder each time the
kitchen door was opened.

It was the night of a threshing I went out in my first set
dance. I was still a schoolboy in short pants, but I had been
watching the dancers for a long time in the houses and at
the Sunday evening dancing deck near Mac's Arch. People
said I had dancing in my feet from the way I used to tap out
the time to the music. I knew the figures of the polka set;
the jig set, I thought, was a little more complicated. I'd never
have had the courage to go out only that my father said he'd
make up the three other men to stand in the middle of the
floor. I stood opposite my father so that he would be my co-
dancer in certain figures of the set. As we stood there we
talked for a while, as was the custom. Then we asked our
partners.

The girls, all eager to shake a leg, had their eyes on the
men on the floor There was no formal request. The women
responded to a nod or a wink. I thought this method a bit
too grown up for me and I walked to the side and said to a

young woman who was a good dancer, 'Will you dance, please?' When the music struck up the women came and stood by the men's right hand. My partner guided me and told me what was coming next in each figure of the set. I became so confident after a while that like my father and the other dancers I added a little embellishment to the step. A bit of heel and toe work. The first time I did this a cheer went up in the kitchen and shouts of ''Tis kind father for you!'

I danced many a set after and pounded many a stone-flagged kitchen at station dance or on threshing night, but the first time I squared out with my father standing opposite me remains the clearest in my mind. Mick and Brian Kelly had a concertina which they played in turn. It was Mick who played for our set, polka tunes for the first three figures and then 'Pop goes the Weasel' for the slide. In this figure my father and his partner danced towards my partner and me. We met them half-way, did some fancy footwork and re-treated. Then forward to meet them again, our right feet hitting the floor in perfect timing. The music gathered speed as we danced to form a square and this went into a swing. The swing, or wheel as it is called, is a tricky thing to get right. The dancer pivots on one foot and wheels his partner around him. Faster and faster we went to keep up with Mick Kelly's music until my head swam as the dancers' faces and the entire kitchen, floor, ceiling and fire went into a mad spin around me. People cheered, egging on the musician. I lost my footing and as the legs were taken from under me, I landed on my backside on the floor, my head still spinning. I must have fainted because I could hear the loud laughter fading as if the wireless were suddenly turned down. My father's face and the faces of the dancers bobbed up and down in my mind's eye, twirling and swirling and turning different colours until they melted into darkness.

Gradually I heard the voices coming back. When I came to I was sitting on a chair and someone was holding a cup of water to my lips. I took a long drink, shook myself and stood up. 'I am all right,' I said to the many enquiries as to how I felt. My father wanted to take me home. No, I was feeling fine. And I was. When the dancers lined out for the final figure in the set I took my place. Mick Kelly didn't race the music and my partner took care that we didn't overdo the dancing. After the dance there was a cup of tea and I was right as rain. On the way home my father talked about what had happened. He was anxious about me, and we decided not to tell my mother. She would be very troubled if she heard that I fell in a faint in my first set dance. She always held I did not have the sturdiness of other young lads of my age and that anything over-strenuous would knock the wind out of me.

They were all in bed when we went home. 'A nice hour to have him out!' my mother complained to my father. I got into bed beside my brother, worn out from the dancing and helping at the threshing. As I fell asleep the events of the day ran through my mind. Stacks of corn going down and the *síogóg* and the straw rick going up. The movement from hand to hand as the sheaves of corn found their way to the thresher, the black smoke belching from the engine and boo-ooo-ooo of the machine mingling with the racing music of Mick Kelly's concertina. I don't remember going to sleep and it seemed as if only minutes had elapsed when my mother called me and my brother for school. When I came downstairs I dashed the cold water on my face and dried myself. I put my lunch in my coat pocket and brought my strap of books to the table. As I sat down opposite my father my mother looked at me anxiously.

'He was talking in his sleep,' she said to my father, 'Did

anything happen to him?'

My father was taking the top off a boiled egg and putting a dust of salt in it. He said, 'These eggs are hardly done, Hannah.'

XII

BY TRAIN TO THE SEASIDE

In my last year at school and coming up to the summer holidays the master put forward the idea of a school outing. 'Hands up,' he said, 'all of you who have been to the seaside?' Not a single hand went up. None of us had ever seen the sea. In fact very few of the older generation had seen it, though my mother, before she married, was on an excursion to Youghal. The sea was a mystery as far as we were concerned and we were delighted when the master announced that he would take the upper classes to Rossbeigh the week before we closed for the summer. He thought that the infants and first and second classes were too small to take them on such a long journey. We agreed with him. And as Sullivan from Ballaugh said to me, 'What do they want there for!' We were very excited at the news. 'Calm down,' he told us. 'This outing will cost money.' There would be the train fare and expenses for the day. Not too much. We could bring our lunch the same as if we were coming to school and get a cup of tea there. He told us what the train fare was and he told us to collect this and bring it to school.

I was up early on the appointed morning. I got into my best clothes, my confirmation suit. Boots, stockings and a skullcap completed the outfit. We had seven and sixpence between my brother and myself, and my father slipped us a two-shilling piece which I think my mother didn't know about. She warned us to be wary of the sea and if we went paddling not to go out too far. My father drove us to Killarney railway station in the pony and trap and we picked up a few boys on the road who didn't have a drive. We were away too early for the train and the time was spent running up and down the platform and counting the boys every now and then to see who was missing. As sure as anything, we said, someone would be late. But they were all there when the train came puffing in from Cork. We were lined up and the master shepherded us into whatever vacant carriages he could find when the Killarney passengers got out. There were no corridors. Each compartment had two seats running the entire width of the carriage. Once you were in and the train moved off you had to stay there, but you could change to another compartment when the train stopped at a station.

It was everyone's first time on a train. We soon got the hang of how to work the leather strap to lever the windows up and down, so that as many of us as could fit were looking out both windows when the train got to Ballyhar. The master got out there and ran along the platform to see that we were all right. He warned us to keep the windows up in case we'd fall out. At Farranfore we all got off and changed to another train. Such excitement! We were like sheep set free from a pen. When everyone had settled down I took my place at the window and watched the guard wave his green flag. He blew on his whistle and with a chug, chug, chug, the train was off. He ran a few steps with the train and then hopped on to the end carriage.

We halted at Killorglin and we promised ourselves that when we were bigger and owned bicycles we would cycle here to the famous Puck Fair held each year on 11 August. At the next station the guard alighted and shouted, 'Molla-hive!' but no one got out or got in. It was full steam ahead to Glenbeigh. All out and into line but a few of us ran forward to have a look at the engine. The furnace door was open and the stoker shovelled coal into the glowing fire, darkening the glow momentarily. When the stoker shut the door the driver put his hand on a lever and a huge jet of steam shot up. There followed a whistle. We got back into line and watched the train gather speed on its way out of the station to Kells and Cahirciveen.

The master, as pious a man as you could meet, marched us out of the platform and into the chapel to say a prayer. Going up the aisle, Sullivan from Ballaugh suddenly genu-flected prior to entering a seat and I, not expecting the genuflection and walking close behind, was thrown out over him. This brought more than a titter from the rest of the class. The master's face clouded at such a display of mirth in a holy place and when we came out we were spoken to very severely. Cafflers, a great word of his, he called us. As we walked down towards the fork in the road where we would turn right for Rossbeigh our hearts sank. A mist started to come down. As we walked along, the fog got thicker and when we arrived on Rossbeigh Strand the master was panic-stricken as our vision was now only a couple of yards. The master was afraid that some of us might stray away and get lost. He collected us in a bunch and warned us to watch him and not to move anywhere unless he was in eye view. We were down in the dumps with depression at having come all the way for a glimpse of the sea and now that we were standing on the strand it was nowhere to be seen.

There was movement in the mist. It seemed to be blown in from the ocean. Sometimes it thinned out and then got so thick you could hardly see the boy next to you. We kept our eyes peeled for the master's black hat, and he kept talking loudly so that if we couldn't see him we knew where he was. Even though a vision of the sea was denied us we were conscious of its presence from the sound of the waves and the smell of the seaside. The master had an idea. We all moved back from where we perceived the sea was and sat on the dry sand and on a heap of stones. He called the roll — everyone was present — and he suggested that we should wait in the hope that the mist would clear, and while we were waiting as it was a long time since breakfast we would eat our lunches. Afterwards he would arrange that we got a cup of tea. As we sat and ate, maybe it was a prayer the master said or maybe it was our visit to the chapel, but the mist got lighter. We took off our shoes and stockings and placed them on the stones and ever so gradually the sea came into view. Only the white surf on top of the waves at first as they chased each other to the shore. When it was clear enough and the master gave the signal, we raced barefoot towards the water's edge. We stopped and watched the waves rush in towards us only to peter out on the sand and flow back into the sea again. The game now was to run after the receding wave and turn quickly so that it didn't catch us as we ran back. We weren't always successful.

The water felt cold at first but after a time we didn't feel it. By pulling up our short pants we paddled in as far as we could and when we got tired of that we raced up the strand and the dry sand stuck to our feet and shins. We found if we sat for a while on the bank of stones the sand dried, little particles of it glistening in the sun, which was now coming out. By rubbing our feet with our hands we got the sand off.

The master said what about a cup of tea. No one found any fault with that. We put on our shoes and stockings and went to an eating house perched over the strand. The lady of the house had a huge teapot as big as a kettle and she filled out a mug of tea for each one of us. There were tables with milk and sugar and chairs where we could sit. The master paid her for the tea and said we could have a second mug if we felt like it. There was a shop at the end of the dining room. This was a chance for us to spend our money. We bought buns, cakes and fat biscuits, and even though it was only a little over an hour since we had our lunch we sat down to a royal feast. Afterwards we bought *tómhaisíns* (conical paper measures) of sweets, bullseyes and NKM toffees.

When we got back to the strand the master talked to us about the sea. He explained the coming and going of the tide and how the waters were influenced by the pull of the moon. He showed us the nets laid out upon the rocks and how a fish working its way through a hole was caught by the fins and held a prisoner. He told us the names of the fish that were netted along the coast, and as the sky cleared the day got warmer and we saw black shapes rolling in the sea. These were porpoises. We wondered would there be any chance we'd see a whale or a shark, but wherever these animals were that day they kept far away from Rossbeigh. Outside where the waves rolled on to the shore the sea was like a sheet of blue glass stretched away to where it met the sky. We were delighted with the variety of seashells and we collected some to bring home to show the smaller members of the family. I got one huge white shell something in the shape of the house the snail carries on his back but miles bigger. The master said if I put it in my ear I could hear the sound of the sea. I brought it home and showed it to the neighbours. They put it to their ears and swore they could hear the sea quite plainly.

The master suggested that we play games and enjoy the sun. Some of the boys had a football but a party of us opted to play ducks off. This was a favourite game which we played at home or by the roadside on our way from school. We selected a big stone with a flat top from the bank and positioned it on the sand. This was the granny. We marked the throwing point about twenty feet back from it. Each player picked a stone about a pound in weight and this was his duck. One boy, a volunteer, placed his duck on the granny. He was the granny man. The others in turn threw their ducks at it, the aim being to knock it off. When a good shot knocked it from the granny there was a mad scramble by the other players to retrieve their ducks from behind the granny. The granny man replaced his duck as quickly as he could, and having done this if he succeeded in touching a boy before he got back to the mark that boy's duck went on the granny. And so the game was played. Every boy as he threw the stone had to shout 'ducks off!' If he omitted to say it the penalty was that his duck went on the granny. It sounds a very dangerous game with all those stones flying, but it wasn't. All the players had to remain behind the mark while the ducks were being thrown.

In time there was an argument. A player claimed that he wasn't really caught before he got back to the mark. This led to a row and the master had to intervene. 'No more rounders!' he said. That was his name for ducks off. We turned our attention to the sea, and noticed that while we were in the eating house and playing ducks off the waves had receded. The water was away out now and we had to race down to it. There were round jelly-like platters on the sand. The master said if we stood on one of those jellyfish we might get a sting. The very big ones which he called Portuguese men o'war were especially dangerous. We were disappointed we didn't see any fish but we did take stock of the birds. They were very different from the crows, pigeons, blackbirds and thrushes which we saw at home. Most noticeable were the white herring gulls with grey backs. They swirled and screamed overhead and landed on the sea. In a way I envied a creature that could walk on land and fly and swim. To my mind that was a form of complete freedom. There were smaller gull-like birds called terns. We had the master bothered asking him the names of the different species. There were very small birds keeping in flocks with a smart walk like a wagtail when they landed and only a short butt of a tail. These were sandpipers.

All in all it was a great day. The one regret we had was that nobody told us about bathing suits. The master never said a word. Maybe he didn't want our mothers going to the expense of buying togs and our using them only once. We would have dearly loved to strip off and dive into the sea and frolic around in the water like we saw some other children do. We really envied them and the bathers running against the high incoming waves and being covered over for an instant and then washed in towards the shore. We saw men swim out to sea and I was as jealous of them as I was of the seagulls who had the best of three worlds. I was firmly planted in one.

It was time to head back for the village of Glenbeigh. On our way past the eating house we saw a woman in a white apron selling sea grass. We decided to invest in a penny-worth. It was of a purple shade and tasted very bitter and salty but after a time we got used to chewing it. We weren't too keen on swallowing the sea grass so when it was all chewed up we spat it out. The master thought our conduct was disgusting. We went back and bought another few pennyworths of it to bring home. When we reached the village I counted my money and with what we had left my brother and I bought sweets for those at home and a barmbrack type cake for my mother. The train came into the station. When the engine stopped, steam seemed to escape through every bit of it. We climbed in and when the porter banged the door shut and the guard waved his green flag and blew his whistle the train chuffed out and we all began to sing. Sullivan from Ballaugh had two lines of a song which went:

We came to see sights that would dazzle the eye,
But all that we saw was the mountain and sky!

And we chimed in with,
'We saw the sea, ah ha, ah ha, we saw the sea!'

When we changed trains at Farranfore my brother and I broke company and joined with the boys in another compartment to see what the fun was like. Not so good. They were mostly a crowd from Minish and one of them got sick after chewing too much sea grass. We had to pull the leather strap very quick so that he could put his head out the window. With every heave we all went 'Aaaah!' to give him encouragement. His brother took umbrage at this and a row developed. They shouted at us, *'Bealach an chabáiste!'* (Ballaugh of the cabbage; market gardening was a sideline by the small farmers there) and we shouted at them, 'Minish hold the bag!' In no time the dukes were up and fists flew. Even the sick man turned from the window and joined in the melée. There would have been skin and hair flying only that the train stopped at Ballyhar. My brother and I got out and joined the Ballaugh crowd in another carriage for what turned out to be an uneventful final run into Killarney.

My father met us with the pony and trap, and when we reached home there was a great welcome for the two heroes. My mother had kept the dinner for us with some roasters (potatoes) sitting on the red embers. We weren't too hungry after all we ate at the seaside, but we didn't refuse a slice of the cake we brought home to my mother. She gave a piece of that to everyone.

When the ramblers came in later the table was cleared and we put out the assortment of seashells we had brought home and two roundy stones of a bluish tinge and shaped like duckeggs. My mother thought it was a pity we didn't hide them until morning and put one of them in an egg cup for my father's breakfast! All the small people got shells and sweets and we showed the men the big shell I brought and just to please us they listened to the sound of the sea. We had enough sea grass to give everyone a piece. The men chewed and twisted their faces at the bitter taste. The man with the famous spit when he had the grass well chewed sent it flying towards the fire where it landed on a red coal. The coal went black and it was a while before it burned red again. We answered all the questions the men asked us about the sea. They remarked among themselves that sea water was very good for pains in the bones. One old man said he had heard of houses where a person could have a hot sea water bath with plenty of oily seaweed in it. He said that a couple of dippings in a bath like that would loosen the stiffest joints. We told him we hadn't noticed such houses.

Young Jack was interested in the tide. The coming and going of the tide was one of the three things which the great Aristotle couldn't understand. The other two things were the work of the honey bees and a woman's mind. 'Na mná go deo,' my mother said (always the women). The storyteller continued, 'There was a man inside in this parish who had never heard of Aristotle or who had never seen the sea or the coming and going of the tide. The same man, Crowley was his name, suffered greatly from pains in his bones. One night at a wake he heard it said that a dip in the sea would bring great relief. Crowley wanted to know would he have to strip off in public and he was told that he would. A very modest man, he had no notion of doing this so he hit on a plan of going to the seaside and bringing home a quantity to bathe in at home in privacy. He set out for Rossbeigh with the horse and car to bring home a barrel of the brine. When he arrived at the seaside there was a fisherman mending his nets. "Are you in charge of the water?" Crowley said. The fisherman not knowing what to make of the question said that he was. "And how much are you charging for a barrel of it?" Crowley asked. "Seven and six," the fisherman told him, saying in his own mind, "They're biting on land today!" Crowley paid him and as the tide was full in he filled the barrel with saltwater and brought it home. He heated a quantity of it over the fire and when night time came he bathed in the barrel. This went on for a week, with Crowley bathing in the barrel every night. True enough it brought relief from the pains in his bones, but as time went on the jizz was going out of the water and he decided to go back to Rossbeigh for another supply. When he arrived at the pier the same fisherman was there. Crowley paid him the seven and six and then looking he saw that the tide was away out. "You'll have to pull out a lot farther to fill your barrel today," the fisherman pointed out. "So I see," says Crowley, "It must be in great demand; 'tis nearly all gone!" '

As we went up the stairs to bed I thought of school tomorrow. No doubt the master would ask us to write a composition about our day at the seaside. If he did I would put into it the story Young Jack told. I lay then in the dark thinking about the day's excursion. When I fell asleep I was in the sea rising and falling with the mighty waves. I was swept away from the shore. Then blessed hour! a huge whale approached me and opened his mouth. I went down into his belly. My shouting as I woke up aroused the house. My mother gave me a drink, saying to my father, 'The excitement of the day was too much for him!'

XIII

The Light of the Fire

The source of light in our house was the paraffin oil lamp. It hung on the wall and was made of tin, with a mirror at the back to reflect the light. The burner had a wick which went down into a container and soaked up the oil. With a twister the wick could be turned up or down. Some lamps had a double burner which gave a far better light. Our lamp had a glass chimney called a globe, though it didn't resemble one except where it bulged out around the burner. Each night my mother trimmed the wick and lit the lamp with a spill from the fire. When she put the flame to the wick it blazed up. Then she turned it down very low until you could hardly see the flame and put the chimney on. This done she turned the wick up very gradually and the flame that had been yellow turned white and filled the kitchen with light. She took a hairpin from her hair and straddled it over the glass at the top of the chimney. This was supposed to attract some of the heat and prevent the chimney from cracking. The only other light came from the fire or the candle in a sconce which lit us to bed.

We loved to sit around the fire before the lamp was lit and watch the glow from the burning turf throw our shadows on the wall. My father had shown us how to cast the silhouette of a rabbit's head and front paws with the fingers of both hands. We often populated the gable and side walls of the kitchen with rabbits and even set them to fight each other. The cat or the small dog, Charlie, loved to sit at the fireside. We used to hold Charlie up and watch his shadow catch a rabbit.

The turf for the fire we cut and saved in Young Jack's bog, but the oil for the lamp we bought in Eugene the Boer's shop. Often I brought it in a can when I was seven or eight. Paraffin has a very strong, unpleasant smell and a gallon of it is very heavy. I had to keep shifting it from hand to hand to relieve the pain in my shoulders. In our house we small people were expected to work from an early age – jobs like minding the cow, feeding the hens and pigs and bringing hay into the cow and pony when they were in their houses for the night. We had to draw all the water for use in the house in buckets and cans: the water for washing from the nearby river and the water for drinking and cooking from a well which was in Sullivans' bohereen a half mile away. The sparkling spring water came out of a spout and the buckets filled quickly. We found that plucking a fan of fern leaf and placing it on top of the bucket kept the water from splashing as we walked. The well was a meeting place for neighbouring women and they sat and talked for a while.

We were nearly always on the go and the seasons brought new work. In mid-summer we helped save the hay when my father bought a field of it at the auction in Danny Mullane's. When things were slack at home we helped in a neighbour's meadow and loved when a gallon of tea and piping hot mixed bread with plenty of fresh butter was brought out from the house in the evenings. Tea always tasted better in the open. When we were working in the bog, a fire was started with sticks and turf, and water from the well put boiling in a can. When it was bubbling the tea was added and then the milk and sugar as the can was taken off the fire. You filled your cup by dipping it in the can and as you sat in the heather drinking tea and eating buttered bread you wouldn't call the king your uncle.

When it came to the time for us to cut a year's firing my father engaged a group, a *meitheal*, of men. They brought their own *sleáns* and turf pikes. We'd set out for Young Jack's bog, where we had rented turbary, early on the appointed day. From the time when I was very young I would plead to be let go with the men that morning. I joined my father in the pony and car, which brought the food for the meals the men would get. The day before the turf-cutting my mother spent baking bread and boiling bacon. Plates of this bacon and rolls of butter with plenty of sharp knifes were put in a covered basket, and the wheels of mixed and white soda cakes in a white cloth bag.

The turf bank was cleared of its top sod the day before by a man with a hay knife, a spade and a length of line. The cleaning measured about two and a half feet. The turf-cutting implement was like a spade with a piece jutting out at right angles on the left hand side called a horn. This *sleán* was very sharp and cut through the soft peat to turn a sod of turf say four inches by four and a foot long. The *sleán*sman stood directly over his work and in one fluid movement he cut down straight through the peat, thrusting out and up as he landed the freshly cut sod on the bank. There a pikeman pitched the sod to another pikeman and he to another who laid the sods in a neat row at right angles to the bank. When it came to a second row the head of each sod lay on the tail of the one before. In time at least three *sleán*smen would be working on the bank, one behind the other, each succeeding

120

one a foot or so lower as if they were on the steps of a stairs. When they got into full swing there was a lovely rhythm to the work, with the sods leaving the *sleán* in quick succession and being pitched by the pikemen to join their brothers on the heather on the bank. Some *sleán*smen sang as they worked or carried on a conversation with the nearest pikeman. The work was hard and on a hot day the sweat poured off the men. Now and again the whole rhythmic machine would come to a halt to draw breath and go on again. My job was to bring a bucket of water from the well and be ready to hand a tin mugful to the thirsty. I remember one *sleán*sman taking the bucket and putting it on his head and drinking from it. The first big break from work came for the midday meal.

On the day of the turf-cutting my mother came to Young Jack's house about twelve o'clock and boiled water. She thought it quicker than building a fire in the bog. Tea was made in a white enamel bucket on which there was a cover. When the men saw her appear in the field below Young Jack's house a cheer went up. A place was selected in the dry heather of the *cois* (a lower level from which the turf had been cut away), and a cloth spread to hold the plates of bacon and butter. The bread was cut and buttered and a slice of bacon put between every two pieces. Milk and sugar were added to the white bucket of tea and the men dipped their cups into it and ate away to their heart's content. There was a rest then as pipes were lit. There were stories and a discussion on whatever were the latest happenings of the world.

My father would not be the first to make a move to return to work. He would leave that to a neighbour who, putting his pipe in the top pocket of his waistcoat would say, 'This won't pay the rent. Back to the grindstone!' In no time the men were in position and the *meitheal* resumed its rhythmic motion. The black sods tumbled from the *sleáns* on to the bank and were pitched by the pikemen into place. The intake of food put the men in good humour and a song was heard drowning the sweeter sound of a disturbed lark which rose in little leaps higher and higher until it became a small speck and its song was lost and we were left with the strains of the ballad 'My Mary of Loughrea'. At four o'clock on the dot my mother would appear again in Young Jack's field with the white bucket. This time there were two large cakes of currant bread. These were sliced and buttered and washed down with cups of hot tea.

The men worked until the bank was cut and a carpet of black sods covered a good half-acre of bogland. The bank was seven sods high and the bottom sod, the blackest and the best, was spread in the cois. The carpet of turf remained that way for some weeks and when a thin crust formed on the sods they were lifted and made into foots. Footing turf is the hardest work I know. As youngsters our backs used to ache from the constant stooping. If we didn't keep our heads down and work hard we'd never be done. I used to pick a place ten or fifteen feet in front and vow I wouldn't lift my head until I had reached that spot. Four sods were put standing by leaning them together and two sods were placed on top. Standing so the drying wind went through the sods and the sun lent a hand in the saving process. From the constant handling of the hard-crusted sods the skin at the tops of my fingers wore thin and began to pierce so that I was driven to take the sod by its under or soft side. The butter-soft peat eased the pain in my fingers but as evening came the blood showed through the skin.

A couple of weeks later the turf was stooked. Three or four foots were put together and a number of sods placed on top. By the dint of drying, the fat sods were now growing thin and shrunk to no more than three quarters of their former size.

Towards the end of the summer the turf was drawn out from the inner bog by the donkey and cart to where there was a metal passageway, and made into a large heap. From here, when the chance came, it was carted home. The turf creel was put on the pony car and Fanny the mare, helped by a neighbouring horse or two, brought the winter's fuel supply to the house. There the turf sods were built into a neat rick, narrowing as it went up and about nine feet high. When the men rambled in as autumn came, they noticed the new turf burning in the hearth. They took up a sod and passed it around and commented on its quality. It was a good year when turf, hay and oats were got into the haggard. God be praised! The talk would turn from the light of the fire to the light of the lamp, and one night Young Jack spoke of God's two lamps in the sky. And he told the men about Copernicus, who was the first man to discover that we went around the sun instead of the sun going around us, which was the belief up to then. Always in top gear when having a go at the Church, Young Jack told us that Galileo, who promoted Copernicus' discovery, was put on trial by the Pope for going against the belief of Ptolemy, which was that the earth was stationary and flat. Galileo was sentenced but because of his age he was confined to his house for the rest of his life. And there are men who still believe the earth is flat, Young Jack maintained, and he told us of a man of the Humphreys who came back from New York. Humphrey, entertaining his neighbours at his father's fireside, filled them with stories of the wonders of America. He claimed he went so far west in the States that he came to the end of the world where there was a cliff, and looking over it he saw all the suns, moons, and stars that pass overhead thrown there in one great heap. 'Only that I had no room in my trunk,' he said, 'I would have brought some of them home to hang up for the Christmas decorations!'

XIV

CHRISTMAS

With the drawing home of the turf the days began to shorten as the sun sank lower in the heavens. The big round cock of hay with a green cap of rushes kept the rick of turf company in the haggard, and a small pile of sheaf oats was stored in the house where the pigs lived during the summer. The hay and oats meant that the cow and the pony were provided for during the winter months. There was turf to keep us warm and with potatoes in the pit, York cabbage in the patch, hanks of onions seasoning over the beam in the workshop and flitches of bacon hanging from the kitchen joists, we humans were sure of our share when the winds blew loud and the rain and the sleet slashed against the window pane. The lamp was lit a little earlier now and the men came earlier to the nightly parliament that was my father's house.

The news of the day over, the men debated the affairs of the nation. Having our own government and the recent Civil War made politics more immediate. In the old days matters of Irish concern had been lost in the largely British business of the House of Commons. In the springtime, great interest was taken in the budget and when there was a sharp rise in the price of tea, beer, spirits and tobacco, our native rulers came in for some castigation. One man, looking into the empty bowl of his pipe, complained, 'John Bull wouldn't have done it to us!' To which a joker added, 'He was a better bull than the bull we have now!'

When it came to the time for us small people to go to bed the men might claim our attention for a little while. It made us feel important when they spoke to us and knew us by our names. They asked us about school. Could we spell lynchpin and consanguinity? I don't know how many times William Murphy told us about the two schoolboys who killed a bull. They lived near Mangerton and one evening on the way home from school they went up the side of the mountain. They continued climbing until they could see their own house, and the cattle in the fields seemed small below them. They came to a place where there was a sizeable round stone balanced on a flag. The stone must be nearly a hundred-weight. They kept rocking it on its bed until it rolled off the flag and sped down the mountain. It gathered speed and went by leaps and bounds. Sometimes it jumped as high as a house until it crashed into a farmer's field and a prize bull looking up from his grazing got the full force of the careering stone between the eyes and he fell down as dead as a doornail.

They avoided the farmer's land on the way home. There they told their father what had happened. He was greatly troubled because the owner of the bull was the crossest man in the barony. The father advised the children, if the farmer was before them on the road to school in the morning, to deny all knowledge of the incident. 'Say you saw no bull,' their father told them. Sure enough the farmer was outside his house in the morning in a tearing temper. He asked them were they up the hill yesterday. The big boy said nothing and the farmer, thrusting his threatening face into that of the small boy who was only about six, said, 'Were ye up the hill yesterday?'

'We were,' the small boy said, 'But we killed no bull though!'

We were terrified of bulls and on the way to school we knew the farmers who kept one and we stayed far away from their land. The darkness frightened us too and my brother and I would go out together for company when we had to bring in turf from the rick in the dark moon. We were afraid of the boodyman (bogey man). We were threatened with him when we were smaller. If we weren't good the boodyman would come with his bag and take us away. The púca we also dreaded. He was supposed to be out at night and according to the men he was a mischievous creature. They described him as a cross between a pony and a hornless goat. He had a flowing beard and big blazing eyes, and with a jerk of his head he could hoist you on his back and gallop off with you through the night. When he came to a black lake he would stop suddenly and send you flying out over his head into the water.

The men used to say with a half-smile and in language we weren't supposed to understand that a man unfaithful to his wife could meet the púca coming home in the small hours after visiting the lady of his dreams. The púca would lever him up on his back and galloping through furze and briars would never draw rein till he landed in the man's yard. He would then stop short and the nocturnal Romeo would go sailing over his head into a dark pool of *múnlach*, a dirty pond of cattle urine and liquid manure. By the time he had dusted himself down all amorous notions would be banished from his mind! The mischievous creature gave a strange laugh when he had done his impish deed. It was a sound something between the neigh of a horse and the bleat of a goat.

I was often roused in the night in the month of November by a loud bellow. I thought it was the púca. No, my father told me, it was a wild stag from Muckross Estate deer park. He had been defeated in his fight for the supremacy of the herd, and would roam the countryside looking for another herd where he could fight again and maybe be king.

Jack o' the Lantern was another being that used to be seen at night. He was a wandering soul and when he was in this world it was said that he committed some heinous crime like killing his father. When he died St Peter wouldn't let him into heaven. He went down to hell and the devil wouldn't let him in there either. Jack pushed his face inside the door and the flames were so great and the heat so intense that his nose caught fire. The devil slammed the door shut and Jack o' the Lantern is going around at night ever since, his nose glowing in the dark. He is seen in marshy places dipping his face in the water to cool his burning nose.

We wouldn't put our heads outside the door on Hallow-e'en. All kinds of spirits were said to be abroad that night. We passed the hours playing games we heard our elders talk about. With a length of string we suspended an apple from the joists. Then the participants had their hands tied behind their backs and tried to take a bite of the apple. A useless exercise until two of us came at each side and by pressing our mouths succeeded in getting bites out of the apple. A variation of this childish innocence was to try to take a bite of an apple floating in a dish of water. When the water spilled all over the kitchen a halt was put to this activity.

Especially for Hallowe'en night my mother bought a barmbrack. Three objects were hidden in the cake: a pea, a stick and a ring. Whoever got the pea would be forever poor. The finder of the stick would be master over all and the one who got the ring would be next to marry. If you put the ring under your pillow you would dream of what your wife would look like.

Now that November was on the wane Christmas was on its way. Throughout the year we dreamed of Christmas. It couldn't come soon enough, and when it came it couldn't stay long enough. We small people worked hard on Christmas Eve helping my father set the tall white candles in crocks of sand, one for every window in the house. Holly sprigs from the huge holly tree which grew at the corner of our house were spiked into the sand around each candle. These sprigs were decorated with flowers which my mother made from coloured crêpe paper. We decked out the kitchen with holly, laurel and ivy, placing it around the window, over the door and on top of the clevvy and the dresser. Two mottoes had been kept from the year before, and were put by the fireplace. One read *Happy Christmas* and the other *A Bright New Year.*

When darkness fell on Christmas Eve the youngest child in the house lit the first candle, my father's large hand making the sign of the cross on his small head and shoulders. The other candles were lit from this and we raced from room to room revelling in the new blaze of light, and out into the yard to see what the effect was like from the outside. We watched the bunches of lights come on in the houses of the townland. They were like clusters of stars as they appeared down the valley and up the rising ground to Rossacrue. Our principal meal was always in the middle of the day. One o'clock was dinnertime, but on Christmas Eve, big Christmas as we called it, the main meal was after the candles were lit. First we all knelt down to say the rosary. Kneeling at the head of the table my mother gave out the prayer in the voice of a high priestess. After the creed she said the first decade. Tonight it was the glorious mysteries. My father said the second decade, I the third and my brothers completed the five decades. Even though my mother's thoughts were soaring on a high plane of piety she didn't forget now and then to look towards the fire to see how the dinner was cooking. Most rosaries ended with, 'Hail, Holy Queen, mother of mercy, hail, our life, our sweetness and our hope,' but ours didn't. When we touched our breasts, calling on the Sacred Heart to have mercy on us, my mother launched into the trimmings:

Come Holy Ghost send down those beams
Which sweetly flow in silent streams.

She prayed for the lonely traveller, for the sailor tossed by the tempest, for our emigrants, for the poor souls, for the sinner who was at that very moment standing before the judgement seat of God and last of all for all of her family:

God bless and save us all,
St Patrick, Bridget and Colmcille guard each wall,
May the Queen of Heaven and the angels bright
Keep us and our home from all harm this night!

Our knees ached as we got up from the floor, and it took my father a long time to get the prayer arch out of his back. We all helped to lay the table. The good tablecloth for Christmas Eve. We were ravenous, but as the eve of a feast was a day of fast and abstinence we, like all our neighbours, had salted ling, a type of cured fish. We saw it opened out flat and nailed to shop doors when we were in town doing Christmas shopping. It was over an inch thick and hanging on the door with the tail at the top, it seemed to be three and a half feet long and two feet wide. The shopkeeper cut squares off it and weighed them. These were put steeping in boiling water the night before to get rid of the salt. When the ling was properly cooked it tasted fine, especially when my mother added to it her own special concoction of white onion sauce. We had whatever vegetables were in season, big laughing potatoes and home-made butter in which you got the barest taste of salt. It was a simple meal but we ate until we could eat no more. We leaned against the backs of our chairs and sighed, 'We're bursting!' 'A nice grace after meals!' my mother said as she started, 'We thank Thee, O Lord, for these Thy gifts . . .' As my father finished the signing of the cross after the prayer he remarked half to himself, 'This house is turning into a monastery!'

After the dinner we helped my mother prepare some food in the cow's feeding tub and my father gave an extra sheaf of oats to the pony. The cow dined alone as her calf had been sold at the November fair at Martyr's Hill. Then we all sat around the fire. The Christmas log, *bloc na Nollag*, as the old people called it, with sods of turf built around it, was catching fire. The green moss still attached to the bark was turning brown and little jets of steam shot out which made the cat sit up. In a while's time when the heat got to the log it aimed sparks at us, and the cat, rising and humping her back, spat in the direction of the log and moved under a chair. The dog ignored the fireworks.

It was time now for my mother to open the Christmas box she got in Reidy's shop where we dealt in town. There was a bottle of wine for herself. That was put away to share with the women who called on small Christmas night, the women's Christmas (6 January). There was lemonade for us and biscuits, and last to come out was a Christmas cake. We had slices of this and cups of lemonade. My father would never look at the Christmas cake. His eye was on the big brown jar full of porter and resting on top of the bin. He wouldn't drink unless he had company. Knowing this, my mother sent me for our next door neighbour to come and sit with us. Our candles lit my way for one half and the neighbour's lit my way for the second half of the journey. Pat Murrell came with a 'Happy Christmas everyone!' and after the exchange of small pleasantries my father took the cork off the brown earthenware jar and poured out two glasses of porter, black as night when it settled, with two creamy collars on top. He handed one to Pat, and he by the way taken by surprise said, 'What's this?' 'Go on take it,' my father urged. ' 'Tis Christmas night and more luck to us!' Pat's face brightened and, lifting his glass, he wished us health and happiness and prayed that we all might be alive again the same time next year.

It was bedtime for us and when my mother went down to the kitchen I came out of the bed and sat on the return steps of the stairs to hear the conversation between Pat and my father. When he got his second glass Pat said, 'I hope we don't go too far with this, like the militiaman in the town of Tralee. He was a raw recruit,' he continued, 'and on pay night he got so drunk that on the way home he passed the barracks and walked out into the country. He sat on a mossy bank and thinking it was his bed he took off all his clothes. He folded his uniform and put it as he thought under the bed. Where did he put it but into a gullet that was there. He lay down and tried to sleep. The night began to freeze and after a while he woke up still tipsy but if the cat went a pound he couldn't find his clothes. He walked off and I can tell you he was feeling the cold now. He kept going until he saw a light in a house in a bit from the road. He threw a stone at the door and it was opened by a young woman. She invited him in.

' "I can't go in," he told her, "I am as naked as when I came into the world!"

' "Well," says she, "There's an old suit of clothes here that won't be wanted any more. My husband is after dying on me!"

'She prayed for the dead and the soldier did so too. Then she threw him out the suit of clothes and he got into it. When he went into the house he saw her husband's corpse laid out on the settle bed. The young woman gave him a glass in his hand. A nice drop it was too and it put the life back into him. As he sat by the warm fire he could hear the young woman talking and laughing with a man in the room.'

'Tch, tch, tch,' my mother said, and began to busy herself around the house.

'Sitting there by the fire,' Pat went on, 'and with the light from a candle, the militiaman was taking stock of his surroundings. Whatever look he gave at the corpse's face he thought he noticed the left eyelid fluttering a bit.'

'The Lord save us!' I could hear mother saying.

'On close examination,' the storyteller said, 'he saw the beads moving that were entwined around the corpse's fingers. All of a sudden the corpse turned his face and beckoned the soldier to come over to him.

' "Bend down your head," he whispered, "until I tell you. I am an old man married to a young woman and letting on to be dead was the only way of finding out if she was unfaithful to me. I have proof now. Do you see that three-pronged pike at the butt of the kitchen? Bring me up that and put it here beside me in the bed!"

' "Go up now," the old man said, keeping his voice low, "and turn down Jack the Cuckoo and my wife out of the room."

'The soldier went to the door of the room and called them

133

and when they came down the "corpse" was dead again.

' "What's wrong?" the young woman said.

' "You know well what's wrong!" says the old man, jumping out of the bed. Jack the Cuckoo gave a gasp and made for the door but the old man put the imprint of three prongs in his backside as he went out. The young woman was going to close the door when her husband said, "Take your shawl and go with him; it will keep the two of ye warm in a gripe!"

'She took the shawl from the peg and went out and as she closed the door after her the old man said to the soldier, "An unfaithful woman is only an encumbrance to a man. You can keep the clothes. I have a good Sunday suit I can wear."

'The soldier had a warm bed for the night and at dawn he set out for the barracks in Tralee. When he went in the militia were drilling in the square and when they saw the raw recruit in a suit miles too big for him they roared out laughing. He was hauled before the captain to explain himself, and he told the story the same as I have told it to you. A major on horseback went out the road to where the soldier described and found the Queen's uniform in a gullet. I forget now what punishment he got. Maybe a week confined to barracks. That's my story. If it didn't happen I can't help it. It wasn't me who thought it up in the first place.'

The story called for another glass and then my father went to the storyteller's house to sample what he had in for Christmas. My mother warned my father as he went out the door not to come back with the signs of drink on him. 'Everyone is for the altar in the morning,' she reminded him. I stole into bed, thinking of the naked soldier going along the road in the dark and the old man lying dead with one eye blinking. It was dark in the room now. All the candles had been quenched except the one in the kitchen window, which would be left lighting all night and the fire kept in.

That was the custom as Sigerson Clifford remembered it:

> Don't blow the tall white candle out,
> But leave it burning bright,
> To show that they are welcome here
> This holy Christmas night.
> Leave the door upon the latch,
> And set the fire to keep,
> And pray that they will stay with us
> When all the world's asleep.

There was a picture of Mary and Joseph in the kitchen. In the clothes they were wearing I couldn't imagine them walking down Bohar Vass in the dark. My mother believed in their presence about us tonight and every night. My father didn't. I once heard him say, 'If that holy pair passed our house on Christmas night, they'd have strayed a tidy step from the road to Bethlehem!'

It was still dark when my mother called us in the morning to go to early Mass. My father was dressed and ready for the road when we came down to the kitchen. We had put our stockings hanging on the crane by the fire the night before. There was a small mouth-organ in mine. In other stockings we found a Jew's harp, a small doll, an orange and a new penny. Father Christmas didn't break his heart but we were satisfied with what we got. Our own father had the pony tackled and under the trap. He was fixing a short piece of candle in the lantern to light us on our way. We all piled in, my mother holding the smallest one in her lap. It was pitch dark and we noticed the single candle lighting in the kitchen window of the houses as we drove along. The road was dry with a slight touch of frost and the clippity-clop of the mare's hooves sounded loud and echoing in the morning air. As we

135

neared the village there was a stream of traffic, the dismal gleam from the candle lamps throwing small pools of light on the road. Some people were in sidecars, some in common cars and a few on the lowly ass and cart. The pony was tied to a bush opposite small Bessie's house. We all climbed out and were warned to stick together and not get lost in the dark. And it was dark, people bumping into each other and then a chorus of greetings as men and women recognised each other. 'Happy Christmas, Con!' 'Happy Christmas, Julia!'

The only light in the chapel was the light from the altar candles and from the shrines of the Blessed Virgin and the Sacred Heart. We couldn't see the rafters of the church and could only barely make out the figures in the big picture of the Assumption into Heaven on the wall behind the altar. The priest and the altar boys looked like shadows when they came from the sacristy. It didn't matter that it was dark because very few read from prayer books; they told their beads. The sermon was very short. The priest wished us a very happy Christmas and said a few words about the nativity and the coming of Christ. Nearly everyone received when it came to holy communion. My father was unaccustomed to the trip from the bottom of the chapel to the altar, but he always went at Christmas and at Eastertime. He and the other men seemed awkward and ill at ease approaching the light at the rails and were happy when they were back in their old place again, kneeling on one knee and telling their beads.

The dawn was breaking as we emerged from Mass. The men stood outside the gate facing the chapel in lines of three or four deep and took out their pipes. The women moved towards their carts and sidecars or collected in bunches talking and exchanging Christmas greetings. The day brightened and the lone vigil candle was still lighting in Pakie Richie's window.

The hunger picked us as we drove home. Except for the few small children we were all receiving and had been fasting since the night before. The kitchen fire was still in and when we added a few sods of turf and sticks it was soon blazing again. Back rashers cut from a flitch of bacon hanging from the joist had been steeping to wash some of the salt away. They were put in the pan with eggs and a circle of black pudding. Slices of shop bread, it being Christmas time, were toasted at the fire and buttered. 'Eat enough now,' my mother advised. 'It will be late before I'll have the dinner ready.'

Darkness had come and all the candles were lighting again before it was on the table, and by that time the postman had called. He was always late on Christmas Day. Jer, the postman, was in high good humour from sampling a little of the season's cheer in the many houses along the way. In the front carrier of his bicycle he had a big parcel for us from our aunts in Dittmar's Boulevard, Astoria, New York. It had small items of wearing apparel, a tie for my father, a colourful apron for my mother, a cotton dress for my sister and knee breeches and jacket with a belt at the back for my brother and me. There was a doll and a small metal brightly painted carriage drawn by two horses with little wheels on their hooves so that we could run the carriage on the table or on the floor. There was a letter, too, with a robin redbreast Christmas card, and when the card was opened out popped three ten dollar bills, which was a small fortune to us. The letter made enquiries about our health and it was signed Mary, Margaret and Elizabeth.

On St Stephen's day we were never allowed out in the wren. Numbers of children, three or maybe four in each party, came to our house and standing inside the door sang:

The wran, the wran, the king of all birds,
St Stephen's day he was caught in the furze.
Up with the kettle and down with the pan,
And give us a penny to bury the wran!

They would get a penny or maybe more if we had it. As well as singing, two of them would lilt a tune and the third would dance a step. They always carried a holly sprig with a coloured paper flower or a dead wren in the middle. The candles were lit in all the windows on the night of St Stephen's day, also on any Sunday nights that fell within Christmas and on New Year's Eve and New Year's Day. New Year's night was the night of plenty. Everyone ate enough on that night. The men used to talk of a custom of hitting a cake of bread against the open door and chanting:

I banish all hunger to the land of the Turks
For a year and a day and every day
From here to eternity!

The feast of the Epiphany was the last night on which the candles were lit. It was believed that water was turned into wine on that night. My father always put a white enamel bucket of water standing outside the door, but the miracle never happened. Small Christmas, the Epiphany was called, and after the supper neighbouring women visited my mother. A portion of Christmas cake was kept for this occasion, and the wine which came in the Christmas box. After a while they would adjourn to another house and it would be late when my mother came home. Next morning the holly and ivy decorations were taken down, the mottoes were put away for another year and what was left of the long candles stored to light us to bed in the long nights ahead.

Candle grease droppings clung to the candles and to the sides of the crocks which held them. We collected the grease and when we worked it between our palms it became soft and pliable. Sitting by the fire we made it into different shapes, little animals and small houses. When we got tired of this, by putting a piece of cord in the middle, we fashioned the lumps of grease into small candles. These we lit in the windows and the tiny light they made revived for us the delight we felt when the tall white candles were first lit twelve days before.

Christmas was gone!

XV

THE APPRENTICE

I left school at fourteen and began my apprenticeship as a carpenter to my father. I was no stranger to the bench. I had been helping him during school holidays for the past few years. Jack Brosnahan was getting out of his time as an apprentice when I started and I was given his place at the bench. At first my time was spent tending my father, holding the board he was sawing or keeping the car shaft in place as it was forced on the body laths, and painting the spoke tenons before they were driven into the wheel stock.

My instinct was to watch how the tradesman did the job and to store up the knowledge against the time when I would be experienced enough to do it myself. There was advice from my father when I came to use the handsaw and the jack plane. I soon learned that to rush the situation gave poor results. The implement had to be given its time to work. There was a rhythm in the movement and sound of the saw or plane when used properly. The correct actions of a craftsman sawing, planing or mortising with the chisel were as fluid as those of an expert hurler on the playing field. In my first year I did much of the easy preliminary work, like removing the proud wood from a wheel spoke with a drawing knife in the fashion of a sculptor's apprentice chiselling away the surplus stone and leaving it to the artist to finish the work.

Now that I was engaged in a man's job it was time for me to get into long trousers. My mother got the suit length in Hilliard's drapery, and I took it to Con the tailor and he measured me for the new suit. A week later I went for a fitting. He put on the sleeveless jacket and with a wedge of white chalk marked where it should be taken in or let out and the positions of the buttons and the pockets. I tried on the basted trousers and felt a little surge of pride as I saw them extended to my feet, covering my knees for the first time since I was born. A week later I went to collect the new suit with the money, as they say, in the heel of my fist to pay Con. The next day was Sunday and I wore the suit going to Mass, and the new cloth cap which I got to go with it. Everyone I knew took notice of me with words of greeting like, 'Well wear!' or 'You're a man now!' Well, I wasn't a man yet. My face was as smooth as the palm of my hand. Next I got a navy blue overalls the same as my father's. They didn't have my size in the shop but my mother cut one down that was many sizes too big for me. In the right trousers leg there was a long slender pocket into which I slid my two-foot rule. At the front there were three pockets for holding nails and the sturdy carpenter's pencil.

Sometimes our work took us away from the bench. This was when my father had the contract of doing the timber work for a new house. There were incentives now to improve rural housing in the form of grants and loans from the new government. If the work was nearby we crossed the fields in the early morning carrying our tools. I ran the leg of the auger through the handle of the handsaw and put it over my shoulder, and carried a bag in the other hand. My father slung a sack on his back with the jack plane, hammers, mallet, chisels and the sharpening stone.

At the farmer's house our first job was to make a temporary bench in the barn or hayshed. Door and window frames had to be ready for the masons to stand in position. Four stonemasons worked together, two outside the wall and two inside as they built against each other. The farmer and his sons tended the masons, mixing lime and mortar and drawing it and building stones to the workplace. The stones were normally found in the farmer's land. Fires were lit on big boulders – you'd see them burning in the night time. The intense heat split the rock right through in several places. By inserting a crowbar in the cracks the men prised the pieces away and broke them into portable sizes with a sledge. When you saw the irregular, jagged shapes thrown at the site you'd wonder how the stonemasons ever built a wall from such unpromising material. The tradesman, casting his eye over the heap, would pick a stone. He knew where the grain lay and by hitting a blow with the sledge on the right place he would split the stone open, revealing two fair faces. Then it was a matter of squaring a bed on the stone and levelling the top and he had two fine building stones. The stone sat on its bed on a layer of mortar with the face plumb at the front and touching the builder's line. The mason took great care when dressing the stone that the top horizontal side never sloped in. This would draw the rain. No tradesman worth his salt built a damp house and even before the joints were pointed with mortar, his work, as he might say to himself, was as dry as paper.

The cornerstone had two faces as near to right angles as didn't matter. They were faced, bedded, placed in position and tested with the plumb-board – as I heard one verbose mason remark, to ascertain their perpendicularity! A line marking the inside and the outside of the wall ran from one gable to the other. The masons built to the lines and from time to time put in a through bond, a stone extending right across the wall which bound the structure together.

About eleven o'clock the men fell out for a smoke. My father and I sat with them, pipes were cleaned out with penknives and the dottle put in the cover. If a pipe didn't pull, a blade of strong grass was run through the stem to free it. Wedges of tobacco were cut from the half-quarter of plug and broken with the thumb and first finger in the left palm. When it was ground to the satisfaction of the smoker he chased stray pieces from between his fingers into the middle of his palm. Then cupping the bowl of the pipe towards the little heap he coaxed the tobacco into the bowl with the first finger of his right hand and pressed it down, but not too hard. Last of all he put the dottle and the ashes in the cover on top, levelled it with his thumb and now he was ready to put a match to it. He drew in the white blue smoke and puffed it out and when he was sure the pipe was properly alight he put on the cover and sat back to enjoy the smoke.

Brian the men called me, thinking that I was called after my grandfather, who was well known to the older men. On the job a young apprentice is at the beck and call of the tradesmen. When they were thirsty I was sent to the farmer's old house for a canteen of spring water. There was a custom among the men of taking advantage of the apprentice on his first day by sending him on ridiculous errands such as to bring the round square and the glass hammer. My father had me primed in this regard and when I was asked to bring the glass hammer I enquired of the mason if the American screwdriver would do? The Americans were reputed to be so anxious to get the work done quickly that they drove screws home with a hammer. An apprentice who was asked to bring a round square went to the public house and got six bottles of stout on tick in the mason's name. Placing the drink in front of the mason he said, 'There's the round, you can square it yourself.'

The men rested for as long as it took to smoke a pipeful. They talked about the trade and about the men with whom they worked down the years. Some of them had been born into the trade and the signs of lime mortar had been on the boots of the menfolk in their families for generations. They talked of the masons being a thirsty tribe. 'Put a pint in a mason's hand,' one man said, 'and with the first swig he'll drive it below the tops of the church windows!' They blamed St Patrick for this state of affairs. It seems the saint came across a group of masons building a house on a Sunday morning and asked them why they weren't coming to Mass. They were Christians now and should observe the Sabbath. Their shoes were bad, they told him, and covered in mortar and not fit to be seen in church. St Patrick gave them money to buy new shoes, which they could do on Sunday morning for the shopkeepers were the last to be converted. 'I'll delay the bell,' he said, 'so that ye'll be in time for Mass.' When St Patrick turned on the altar to give the sermon he looked round the congregation but there was no trace of the masons. Later, coming up the street, the saint heard the sound of singing coming from a certain establishment. Going over, he looked into the public house, and there were the masons inside paralytic on the price of the shoes. 'I'll say nothing,' St Patrick said, lifting his eyes to heaven, 'I'll leave them to God!' 'And that's why,' one man said as he eyed his own footwear, 'you'll never see a good shoe on a mason. And another thing: there never was a man of them yet but wouldn't drink Lough Erne dry!' Two of the men working on that house would go on what was termed 'a tear' on Saturday night and wouldn't be seen again until Tuesday morning.

Back at the bench in the hayshed I helped my father. When we had the front and back door frames made, complete with fanlights, we turned our hands to making window frames. In that style of house, and it was the same style that was being built everywhere, there were five windows at the front and five at the back. Window sashes had to be made to fit the frames and a panel door for the front. The back had a plain boarded and ledged door. The old farmhouse was long and low and thatched and sat snugly in a hollow about half a field away. It had two rooms and a loft reached by a ladder from an enormous kitchen. When I got older and developed an eye for the fitness of things, I realised how much better the old house looked hugged by the hillside than the new one bleak and alone on the higher ground. I realised too that the farmer didn't want to go to the trouble of rethatching the old house every couple of years and good thatchers were getting scarcer as the years went by. The farmer and his wife wanted to get away from the yard where the cowhouse, piggery and stable were clapped up to their front door. The manure heap was under their noses. They wanted more space and a view from the front door. A parlour, too, was in the fashion and an upstairs, and all that glass of ten windows was a great attraction. I often thought that if the government grant and loan were given to add a new room to the existing house, to alter the entrances to the out offices so that the animals and the manure were kept away from the front door, and train new thatchers, how much better the countryside would look.

The turkeys, some say, put an end to the thatched house. As geese were falling out of favour for the Christmas dinner large flocks of turkeys were being kept by the farmer's wife. They were well fed to put up the poundage on the Christmas scales. When the turkeys got the full power of their wings to rise in the world was their sole ambition. The roof of the house was as high as they could go, where they scratched and scraped to their hearts' content, damaging the thatch and letting the drop down into the farmer. Men who couldn't afford new houses covered the thatch with corrugated iron. My father was an expert at this operation. Many is the time I helped him place the rafters over the existing thatch, bind them with laths to the old roof, nail on the purlins and stretch the sheets of zinc on them. When finished, the house didn't look as well as when it had its amber coat of new thatch, but because of the situation and the way it blended with its surroundings it looked better than the new one. Leaving on the old thatch ensured that the house was warm and snug and the rain couldn't be heard pelting on the corrugated iron. In a few years' time when the zinc was painted tile-red, the house sat in harmony with the out-buildings and the hayshed.

In the hayshed where my father and I worked on our first day, the sun was now high in the heavens and our tummy clocks told us that it must be near dinnertime. The woman of the house came to the door and cohooed and beckoned in our direction. The dinner was ready. I ran to tell the masons and we all trooped into the huge kitchen of the house.

The deal table was in the centre of the floor, and the four masons, my father and I and the farmer and his son sat around it. Like the last supper it was an all male affair. There was a bageen cloth on the table. This was a couple of flour bags opened out, sewn together and washed and ironed, but the brand of the flour was still plain to be seen. 'Pride of Erin. 120 lbs.' The keeling over of a pot of potatoes soon covered the brand. The stray Champions which rolled off the table we caught in our laps and added them to the mound of laughing goodness from which steam ascended to the black roof. The farmer's wife and good looking daughter saw to our needs. Theirs was a friendly welcome and a friendly word for each one. Plates of home-cured bacon almost sweet to the taste were placed before us with lashings of white cabbage. Because there was only one fire the bacon and cabbage were cooked in the same pot. The bacon greased the cabbage so that it glistened when the light fell on it in the plate. The meal would be the same tomorrow and the day after except that now and again turnips replaced the cabbage as a vegetable.

There was a bowl of milk before each man, buttermilk which the men loved, or skimmed milk which had thickened almost to the consistency of jelly. As they drank this it left white moustaches on the men's faces. I often meant to count the number of potatoes a working man would eat. It wouldn't rest at a half dozen. A spud was selected from the heap, peeled with the knife and halved on the plate before it found its way to the mouth and thence to the digestive department. All the men blessed themselves before eating but some kept their hats on during the meal. First the men talked about the potatoes they were eating, and there were remarks like, 'They're good everywhere this year.' They knew that this particular variety had come off boggy ground because of the clean white skin. They knew by their shape that they were Champions. They spoke of other varieties, of Irish Queens, British Queens, Epicures, and a new kind making its appearance called Golden Wonders. They discussed the methods of cultivation, the difference between drills and ridges, first and second earthing and spraying against the blight. Then they turned their attention to the bacon. A tasty bit was the verdict. The man of the house told them he had added a

dust of saltpetre to the common salt when curing, which gave
it an extra flavour. The cabbage escaped comment except that
one man wanted to know if it was York.

By the fire sat an old lady I took to be the farmer's mother.
She wore a coloured shoulder shawl held with a brooch at
the front. She had a white apron and on her head a lace affair
with a starched linen front, a little like a nun's wimple, what
my mother used to call a dandy cap. By her side she had a
black walking stick with a crook. She reminded me of the
bishop as he sat on the altar the day I was confirmed. She
was very shy of the strange men the first day. She saluted
each one courteously as he went to shake her hand. But as
the days went by she blossomed out and in the end held her
own in our mealtime conversation. She talked to the older
men about the days when she was young, about the hardship
when but a young girl she worked as a servant for a big
farmer. Up at cock-crow and milking her share of eighteen
cows. She helped the farmer's wife with the housework, the
butter-making and the boiling of food for the animals. She
drew water from the well in huge buckets until her arms were
nearly pulled out of their shoulder sockets. She had to do
the work of a man in the fields, and watch herself from the
amorous advances of the farmer when they got out of sight
of the house. She worked for a whole year for a ten pound
note. Of course she had her board and she slept in the loft
over the stable. At night she used to pull up the ladder after
her so as to be out of reach of her boss and the servant boy.
Some of the men took these accounts to be a form of
bravado because I saw them winking at my father.

Despite the hardship of the few years she gave in service
she wouldn't exchange her young life for that of Queen
Victoria. She relished the memory of her days at school. Her
mistress was a real lady and her father used to doff his hat

to her the same as if she was the priest. Her youthful days
before she went out working were all sunshine. Strolling by
the river bank, gathering hurts (whortleberries) in Merry's
wood in October or courting on the grassy slopes of the
railway on a Sunday evening fair; Sunday nights too at the
dances in a neighbour's kitchen. The tapping on the flagged
floor to the music of the Kerry slide and the mad wheel at
the end of the hornpipe. She was back in those days again
as she lilted or sang a verse of one of the songs which used
to punctuate the set dances.

When the roses bloom again down by the willow,
and a robin redbreast sings his sweet refrain,
For the sake of auld lang syne,
I'll be with you sweetheart mine,
I'll be with you when the roses bloom again.

When her brother married in his small farm the dowry his
wife brought him came to her and enabled her to marry into
this house, where she met a lovable man, God be good to
him, and where she never saw a hungry day.

When I looked around the old kitchen it reminded me of
the house where my grandfather was born in Gallaun. The
same small window in a wall that seemed three feet thick.
The open door to allow in the light, and the closed half-door
to keep the small animals and the fowl out. Two hens and a
cock perched on the half-door as we were eating on the first
day and seemed to complain bitterly that they were hungry
and why weren't they getting something. With a 'hurnish'
from the woman of the house and a flapping of wings they
were gone. About three feet out from the fire wall and at a
person's height there was a round beam, the thickness of a
telegraph pole, extending from side wall to side wall. Over

the fire and resting on the beam there was a six-foot wide wickerwork canopy tapering up to the chimney outlet. It was plastered over and whitewashed like the beam and the walls of the kitchen. At each side of the canopy the beam was boarded into the fire wall so that there was a place to store things. On one side was the donkey's tackling and on the other side the harness for the horse. The door to the bedroom was at the side of the fire and at the other end of the kitchen in the middle of the wall was the door to the second room very often used as a dairy. High up on the same wall was another door reached by a ladder, to the loft where the son slept.

The settle, which was a bed at night, was placed by the back wall a little down from the fire and below it the dresser. These were brightly painted in blue and white and the dresser, even with the dinner plates and drinking bowls in use, carried a fine array of shining delf. Between the window and the front door and high on the wall was an open-shelved piece of furniture called a clevvy. A hanging piece, it carried a display of tin mugs, lustre jugs and highly polished saucepan covers on hooks. Directly under it stood the separator, screwed down to the gravel-filled box in which it came from Sweden. Alpha was the name at the side. There was a large bowl at the top into which the new milk was poured and as the handle was turned the milk went through the machine and cream came out one spout and skimmed milk out the other. The separator replaced the broad shallow pans in which the milk was set and left for the cream to come to the top and in a short time it too was replaced by the travelling creamery.

In olden times and indeed still in some houses there was a coop beside the back door in which fowl were kept at night. It was a splendid piece of furniture, painted the same as the dresser and the settle. It had two compartments into which a dozen hens could be packed, six above and six below. The shutters were slotted and through them the hens poked their heads and carried on a constant cluck-cluck until the lights were put out and everyone went to bed. The cock was never cooped up. He sat on top or perched high up on the crossbeam. At the crack of dawn he flapped his wings and crowed and the hens clucked so that there was little peace in the house until someone got up and released them into the yard. The rafters were blackened from maybe a century of smoke but for three feet before they entered the walls they were whitewashed. These were the rafters that echoed to the loud cries of sorrow when there was a tragic death in the family, or in happier times to the sound of music at a wedding dance or to the tingling of the consecration bell at the station Mass.

There was a notion creeping in lately of having a cup of tea after the dinner. The older men wouldn't hear of this. They preferred to wait for the tea break at about four o'clock. I drank the tea and so did my father, while the masons smoked their pipes. After a suitable lapse of time to allow the food to settle, one of the masons, much to the farmer's relief, got up with a 'This'll never pay the rent' and the men walked back to the building site and my father and I went to our temporary workshop in the hayshed. Everyone was in good form after the dinner. We could hear the masons singing as they worked. They were expert tradesmen and in a matter of days they had the walls high enough to receive the joists for the upper floor. When the walls reached the eaves and the two gables were built, my father put on the roof. The rafters, each two coupled, had been made on the ground and hoisted into position with a bird's beak shape at the end of each rafter finding a resting place on the wall plate. With the slating machine I punched holes in the bluish-purple Bangor slates. The men tending drew the slates to my father and with some help from me he covered the two sides of the roof in one day. The chimneys were lead-flashed, the roof ridged and the eaveshoots and downpipes fixed in position.

We glazed the sashes and put them in the window frames. I loved pressing the soft putty between my hands and if it got too soft I added whitening to bring it to its proper consistency. My mind often wandered and, making small animals with the putty, I populated my corner of the bench with cows, horses and sheep. A shout from my father would bring me back to reality and I would proceed to bed the sash rebate with soft putty to receive the glass. With the sashes glazed, the weather was excluded from the house and the woodwork of the inside began. First the timber floors were put down. I became an expert at driving black brads shaped like a 7 with a long leg into the boards. The last blow of the hammer had to be so timed that the head went below the surface without leaving the mark of the hammer on the board. If I did this I'd get a rap of my father's hammer handle on the knuckles. He hated slovenly work. He was a kindly man and lost his temper only if I did something extremely stupid like this. He expected me to learn the trade by watching him rather than telling me or demonstrating the work like an instructor. Only if I persisted in doing something wrong would he take the tools from me and show me how to do it the correct way. But Rome wasn't built in a day and it took much practice and hours of hard work before I achieved proficiency in the use of the woodworking implements. I often spotted him watching me out of the corner of his eye and if I got something dead right a smile of satisfaction would light up his face.

When the floors were down we made a workbench inside

the house and here we made the staircase. A simple knowledge of geometry was needed to work out the rise and the
going of each step. The two heavy string boards which
support the steps were marked and chased to take the treads
and the risers. My father with the tenon saw cut into the
wood and I with the chisel and mallet scooped out the
channels. Chips flew before the chisel as I did the rough
work. My father finished the channel with the paring chisel
to the correct depth. The steps, risers and treads were glued
and wedged and with a newel post at the top and the bottom
the staircase was manoeuvred into position. I was the first to
run up and down. Seeing my obvious delight at treading on
my own or partly my own handiwork, my father as he stood
back admiring the structure said, 'Will you ever grow up!'

Our next job was to erect the partitions to divide the
rooms upstairs. These partitions were sheeted with ceiling
boards, four and a half by a half inch and 'veed' and rebated.
With the same boards we ceiled the rooms upstairs and the
parlour below. The kitchen joists were left bare. From these
would hang the flitches of bacon when the farmer killed a
pig in October or November. The window-sills were put in
and the reveals boarded. With the architraves in position
around the doors and windows the woodwork of the house
was complete, but before we were entirely finished all the
exposed wood was sized, stained yellow ochre and then
varnished. The masons had put in the concrete window-sills,
put down the cement floor and plastered the walls. When
the plaster dried out the farmer and his family left their snug
house in the hollow and took possession of their castle on
the hill.

The last time we all sat down to a meal in the farmer's old
kitchen the talk turned to the new system that was creeping
in of building houses with poured concrete. The masons

realised that houses built with stone would soon be a thing of the past. There was a sadness in their voices as they spoke of their ancient craft, a trade that went back to the legendary Gobán Saor who built the round towers and was so respected that he, the bard and the storyteller sat at the same table as the king.

XVI

FUGITIVE

The hayshed in which we had our temporary workshop was built by my father. The rick thatched with green rushes and the round stacks of oats with their pointed roofs looking like an African village were no longer seen in farmers' haggards. Haysheds to hold hay and corn were going up everywhere when I started my apprenticeship to carpentry. My father was in great demand for this type of work and had the reputation of building a hayshed in a day. He had to in order to cope with the call on his services. But he had to have help. The farmer, his sons and maybe a neighbour or two had the holes already dug and were in readiness in the early morning to stand the poles in position and pack the earth firmly around them.

Wall plates were secured to the tops of the poles, the roof couples made and by the break for the midday meal the skeleton of the structure stood in place, crying out to be covered with corrugated iron. It was a very mean man who wouldn't have a few dozen of stout in the house for an occasion like this. The men had a bottle each with their meal instead of a bowl of milk. After we had eaten our meal the sheets of zinc were stretched on the purlins and I helped my

155

father nail them down. For the next few hours an almighty din of metallic sound filled the countryside and before the sun sank at the end of a long summer's day the roof was capped and two sides and one gable were sheeted and secure. When my father had driven the last nail home he threw down the hammer and struck his hands together as much as to say 'I've done it again!' If there was a bottle of stout left he got it and the men praised him and said no other man alive could have accomplished what he did in one day. When the farmer gave him the money which was agreed to, after a little bit of humming and hawing, my father put it in his pocket and when we came home he gave it to my mother and she put it in the small box with the sliding top. When he was paid for a smaller job in the workshop he kept the money to buy a half-quarter of plug tobacco, or for the security of feeling a pound or two in his pocket if he met a man in town and they went for a few drinks.

Haysheds weren't long up when they became trysting places for courting couples on their way home from all-night dances. Indeed they often housed two or three couples locked in fond embraces. We were told that a farmer in the dark of a winter's morning, collecting an armful of hay for his cows, unknown to him pulled the slip-on shoes off a young woman's feet and carried them buried in the hay to the cattle shed. She uttered no syllable of protest because she and her partner were afraid of being caught in such a place. The owner would go out of his mind if he knew the hayshed was being used for such a purpose. Morals didn't trouble him. What did bother him was the lighting match of a cigarette smoker. The winter feed of corn and hay for his stock could go up in flames. When the coast was clear we presume the lass and her lover stole out, very careful not to arouse the dog, and she went home barefoot.

I slept in our hayshed for nearly a week one time and my parents didn't know I was there. This is how it came about. After a few years working with my father and doing a man's share I was in my view a man and should be doing the things young men were doing. One of these was going on Sunday nights to house dances. My mother, who was the boss in these matters, didn't mind but she objected to my staying out until three or four o'clock in the morning at all-night dances. Dancing in an overcrowded, unventilated kitchen with a blazing fire in the hearth and coming out into the freezing winter air covered in perspiration could result in a very bad cold. Getting wet going to a ball night and leaving the clothes to dry on my back often gave me a cough so severe that my mother likened it to the sound of two stones striking together. Many people died of consumption around where we lived. In one case a whole family was wiped out.

'You'll never stop,' she used to say to me, 'until you bring it into the house to us.'

Her brother Mike had died of tuberculosis a few years before and my racking cough filled her with horror.

But I went against her wishes. I had met someone for whom I had a true wish, and she was the attraction which drew me to any dance where I thought she might be. Because I was a good dancer she liked being asked out in a set dance with me. There were two kinds of set dance, a jig and a polka. Each comprised three figures and a slide, but the jig set ended with a hornpipe tune and the polka set with a reel. I used to whirl my girl like mad in the wheel of the hornpipe, but I never lost my footing as I did the first time I went dancing. Jude was slim and fair-haired and her blue laughing eyes were before me every waking hour. It took a long time before she agreed that I could walk her home, but at last when she fell in with my wishes I was in the seventh heaven. Holding hands was the only liberty she allowed and after a few words at her father's gate she was off like lightning into the house.

She kept me on tenterhooks for ages. The more she resisted my well intentioned advances the more my heart ached to hold her in my arms, if only for a single minute. The more I thought about it the more I feared the muddle I would make of the whole thing if it ever came to pass. I wasn't eating, my mother said, and my father had to call me from my daydreams to attend to the work in hand. Walking in the pitch dark one night coming from a dance, Jude and I bumped into a horse that was standing stock-still in the middle of the road. She held on to me because of the fright she got and I threw my arms around her to comfort her. The horse trotted off and my mouth found hers, and oh glory, the blood surged through my veins and bells and gongs and a delightful commotion took over my head. She was taken aback at my ardour but it was the start of many a blissful sojourn as we backed an oak tree close to her father's house. She would never go into a hayshed or lie on the soft grass on the slope of the railway. We met on Sunday evenings and walked the quiet stretch by the river or picked whortleberries in Merry's wood in October whose juice stained our mouths a bluish purple. I loved her but I was never sure if she had a true wish for me.

One night the stepping stones were dry as we crossed the wide river to a dance at Griffiths, but it rained so heavily during the night that they were covered when we were coming back. By the mercy of heaven the sky had cleared and the moon shone brightly, and we could see the tops of the stepping stones under maybe three or four inches of water. Rather than go the long way around by Gortacoosh we decided to cross the river. We took off our shoes and she gave me her stockings to put in the pocket of my body coat. I put my socks in the other pocket and we set out. The water was freezing cold and we doubled back a few times. Finally taking courage, we faced the river. I went first and when I reached a step I helped her to gain a foothold beside me. Half-way across, the surface of the stepping stones became very uneven and it was harder to get a firm footing. Nervousness on her part turned to sheer fright when she saw how far more we had to go. I had often seen the river when it was nearly dry and I knew the height of the stepping stones. If we fell off them, I told her, we wouldn't drown only get very wet. The river was fordable at that spot and didn't run very swiftly. We were quite safe. By the dint of assurance and reassurance she soldiered on from step to step until we reached the other side. What were tears on her part turned to laughter. We threw back our heads and roared merriment into the night. We ran barefoot up and down the bank till we got the blood in circulation again. As our feet were wet we put on our shoes barefoot and strolled along. We stopped and hugged and talked and hummed and sang till we came to her father's gate. I doubled back home and the cock crew as I went in the door.

My mother was awake and scolded me severely for being out so late. She lost her temper as she was wont to do when I came in at what she called an unearthly hour. My smaller brothers and sisters woke and began to cry, and my father, ever a man of peace, pleaded with my mother to wait and thrash it out in the daytime. Half of my mind was savouring the happiness I had experienced walking from the river with Jude in the moonlight and the other half was revolting against a scene like this which was ruining the memory of that enchanted hour. My temper was as quick as my mother's. Everyone said I was taking after her. I shouted back that I was a man now and that I would come in any time I liked. This unexpected outburst made her cry bitterly. To think that the son she had reared would shout at his mother. To think that he had so little respect for her and for his small brothers and sisters to stay out all night God only knows where, or in what company, and to come home now at cockcrow and turn the house into a place of turmoil.

'Do you hear him?' she said to my father. 'He'll come in any time he likes. He can come in any time he likes but it won't be into this house!'

Now that her temper had taken possession of her she was in full flight vocally, her language almost poetic as she assailed me for being an ungrateful son. A son, for all she knew, lost in the depredation of sin. How could there be luck or grace in a house where a son had turned his back on God and succumbed to the temptations of the devil! I hung my coat on the newel post of the stairs and the daylight poured through the window as I climbed up to bed. Even as sleep claimed me I could still hear my mother sobbing and speaking to herself and praying the verses she often prayed:

> Angel of God my guardian dear,
> To whom God's love commits me here.
> Ever this night be at my side,
> To light and guard to rule and guide!

As I fell asleep, a resolution was forming in my mind. I would leave this house . . . yes, I would leave . . . I would go . . . I was dreaming and a torrent was raging in the river and sweeping my loved one from my arms. I struggled to save her but my head went under and the water poured into my lungs. Slowly darkness filled my head and the world slipped away from me. My mother was there in my dream. She stretched out her hand to me. She was smiling. 'A *leanbh*' (my child), she said, 'I love you!' Then through my open mouth my soul in the shape of a butterfly escaped from my body and hovered over the river. I could see the body my soul had left drifting with the flood. Beside it was the body of my sweetheart, Jude, her fair hair flowing with the stream. And as I called out to her a white butterfly came out of her mouth and fluttered up towards me. We winged our way to paradise and strolled together through flower bedecked fields. We had shed our wings and walked again with earthly bodies. We saw the bearded saints and St Joseph was making a wheel, our Lord a young man holding the spoke as St Joseph drove it into the stock. Mary brought tea to them in the workshop. Angels flew overhead and God when he appeared was a dazzling light . . .

The sound of the blind going up woke me and the sunlight flooded into the room. 'Are you going to get up at all today?' It was my father and he didn't sound cross as he added, 'You'll be the death of your mother!' And, I thinking of the resolution that was forming in my head as I went to sleep, said, half under my breath, 'I won't be troubling her long more!' As I dressed and went downstairs I recalled the strange dream I had and the vision of my mother smiling and holding out her hand to me as I drowned. She was standing in the middle of the kitchen floor holding out a pair of girl's stockings which she had found hanging out of the pocket of my coat. My whole being went into a jelly at the thought of what she and my father would think. There was a look in my mother's face I had never seen before.

'What have you done?' she demanded. 'Have you shamed us?'

My love for my mother was stronger than that for my father. I treasured every thought of how she cherished us when we were young. I couldn't live under the same roof with a mother whose love had turned to ice, a mother who believed that I had done something that was terrible to her way of thinking. These thoughts went through my mind in a flash as I explained to her what had happened.

'Coming home from Griffiths' dance,' I told her, 'the flood was over the stepping stones and we took off our shoes and she put her stockings in my pocket.' My mother wanted to know who I was with and I told her it was Jude Scanlon. 'Our feet were too wet to put on our stockings when we reached the bank. We laced on our boots and forgot to put on our stockings after. If you don't believe me, see in my other pocket and you'll find my socks.'

She gave me a look and I didn't know whether it said, 'I believe you,' or 'I don't want ever to see you again.' I went back upstairs and put a few things together and threw them out the window. On my way down I took my coat, then went out of the house, hopped on my bicycle and rode away. As I pedalled on, tears of temper blinded me and I had no notion of where I was going. What was driving me on? Was it the bitter pang inside of me of being rejected for something I didn't do? I knew from my catechism and from the sermons of the holy fathers at the missions what was wrong, but I hadn't done anything. Jude Scanlon and I were as pure in our love as the driven snow. I thought again of the dream I had of being in heaven with her. To be dead and that dream a reality was what I wished for now; to go on forever walking hand in hand through the flower-filled fields of paradise.

A magpie perched on a birch sapling let out a raucous screech at me. Mocking me. It was unlucky to see one magpie. One was for sorrow. I cycled on through the next village and the next. I had had no breakfast and I wasn't hungry. I stopped in Millstreet, almost twenty miles from home. The church was being repaired. I left my bicycle against the gate and went in to look at the work. Who should I see but Dan Cronin, who used to build houses with my father. He was surprised to see me and wanted to know where I came out of. I told him that there was a row at home and that I ran away. He laughed. 'All part of growing up,' he said. 'I ran away from home myself but I was soon back when the hunger picked me.' The hunger was beginning to pick me now.

'Was it a woman?' he asked. 'Ah, but you are too young for that caper!'

'Maybe it was!' I admitted, a manly tingling surging through my boyish frame.

'I'll ask the boss if he has anything to do for you and maybe you'd be over your *tormas* (sulk) in the evening.'

He went and asked the contractor and I was taken on to help a carpenter who was making a framed and sheeted door for the sacristy. I had no tools and he was lazy enough to let me use his. Tradesmen are noted for their attachment to their implements and stonecutters have been known to bury their favourite chisels in the mud floor of the workplace if they are going away for a few days.

I mortised the stiles of the door and the carpenter cut the tenons on the cross pieces. He was pleased with my work. He wouldn't let me bead the sheeting as I hadn't used a bead plane before. The top of the door had a Gothic head and I had a lot of sawing to do to shape the head from a wide plank. I did the rough work and the carpenter finished it. At the midday break Cronin remarked that people who run away from home don't have any money.

'I have a ten bob note that's in two halves. I don't know how I tore it. If you can fix it,' he said, 'you are welcome to it.'

I was at my wits' end to know how I could piece it

together until I thought of the gummed strips torn from a stamp sheet. I went to the post office and there on the window-sill were plenty of them. I licked a long strip and put it at the back of the ten shilling note with half the strip protruding. Then very carefully I matched the two pieces of the note together. It looked perfect on one side and that was the side I kept up when I paid in a small café for tea, bread and butter and a plate of ham. The whole thing came to a half crown. I brought the change back to Cronin. He took only the price of two pints and left me the rest.

That evening with the door nearly finished, there didn't seem to be any more work for me. The contractor gave me five shillings. I got on my bicycle and without thinking I headed for home. It was dark when I got near the house but I couldn't get myself to go in. The *tormas,* as Cronin called it, hadn't worn off. I hid my bicycle in the lime kiln and went into our own hayshed. Even though it was late spring there was still a pole of hay there. After being at an all-night dance the night before, I was worn out for the want of sleep. In no time I was fast asleep and it was the cock crowing in the morning that woke me. I stole out in the half dark and cycled away. Passing a neighbour's house I saw that they were up and I went in. Paddy, the man of the house, was someone I could trust and I told him that I had left home and asked could I lie low for a few days. I stayed, and as I was in the house and idle he went to town and got ceiling boards to ceil the room. The stations were due next month. He had a good sharp saw and a hammer and that would do me to carry out the job. When the boards arrived I fell into work, Paddy tending me and holding up the board at the far end until I had nailed it in place.

In my innocence I told him and his wife Mary about my trouble at home and the situation that led to it. Paddy had often crossed those flooded stepping stones himself when he was courting Mary and they had often taken off their shoes and stockings. Paddy thought it a very comical occurrence going in home with the stockings of the girl next door in my pocket. He laughed heartily at it but it was no laughing matter for me. Still his attitude helped to thaw out the ice of ill-feeling between me and home just a small bit. I took my time with the job of ceiling the room. There were a few more things around the house which needed the attention of a tradesman and I did these as well.

Each night I came back home but as I couldn't face in I slept in the hayshed. There were small insects in the hay which worked their way inside my clothes and irritated my skin. How I longed for my own bed and the pleasure of changing my clothes and putting on a clean shirt. When I was sitting by the fire in Paddy's kitchen the heat aroused the insects next to my skin so that it was a torture to keep from scratching myself. I made excuses to go out and rub my back to the cornerstone of the house and give myself a good shaking.

Paddy pulled my leg about Jude Scanlon and it was a nice sensation hearing her name mentioned. She was never for one moment out of my thoughts. As Paddy said, 'You have it bad! You are only a *garsún* (boy) yet. You will put many more women through your hands before you settle down.'

I was seventeen and I hadn't my trade fully learned but no matter how long I had to wait to marry, Jude would be the woman I'd choose to spend my life with. I was firmly convinced of that.

'If you went knocking at Scanlons' door looking for Jude's hand at your age old Scanlon would put the dogs after you,' he laughed. Then he talked about Jude's father, in his lighter moments as comical a man as there was in the parish. I knew him well. He was the life and soul of any house where people gathered. Paddy heard him say that when he was courting Jude's mother he went to ask her father for her hand. He boasted that his was a love match, which was unusual at the time. Her father offered him a drink and a pipe of tobacco, and Scanlon in an effort to make a good impression said, 'I don't drink, smoke, play cards, go with women, bet on horses or take an active interest in politics.'

'Tell me,' the girl's father enquired, 'Do you ate grass?'

'Oh no, I don't,' said Scanlon.

'In that case,' he was told, 'you are not fit company for man or beast!'

Scanlon, reaching out his right hand for the glass and his left one for the pipe, said, 'Now can I marry her?'

Suddenly Paddy changed his tune and said that Mary and he had humoured me along for most of a week and that it was time for me to go back home. 'I am a friend of your family,' he told me, 'and I would be failing in that friendship if I didn't urge you to return to your parents. Your mother will be out of her mind wondering what has happened to you. The *tormas* [Cronin's word again] should be worn off you by now.'

I thanked him and his wife for their kindness to me and went out into the black night. I took my bike and instead of riding off I walked with it through the dark, mulling in my head Paddy's words. I wasn't a man yet, no more than a boy trying to come to grips with growing up and coping with the miracle of being in love. I thought of what my father and mother must have felt all the days I was away. A warmth for my mother was burgeoning in my breast. The *tormas* was wearing off. I could go back tonight and sleep between clean sheets. I hopped on my bike and rode like a madman through the dark till I came to our own gate. I put the bicycle in the hayshed and went to the door of the house. Passing the window I saw that the men, the nightly ramblers, were still sitting in the kitchen. This would be the wrong time to go in. I waited in the hayshed until I heard them going. At the sound of the last 'goodnight' I went and opened the door and peered into the kitchen. There was no one there but my father. He had his boots off and was hanging his socks on the crane. As he reached for the tongs to rake the fire I said 'hello' very softly.

Without lifting his head he took the red coals and half-burned small sods and buried them in the ashes.

'I came back,' I said, in an effort to fill the painful silence.

'If you were younger,' he replied, 'I suppose I'd have to take the stick to you. Have you anything to say for yourself?'

'I'm very sorry,' I blurted out, 'for upsetting you and my mother. Where is she?'

My mother was in bed. I lit the butt of a candle, put it in the sconce, and went into the bedroom. I put the candle on the chimney-piece and, seeing me, she sat up in bed and looked at me for a while. I expected to get a telling off. But no. Suddenly her face softened and she smiled. '*A chuisle mo chroí!*' (my heart's pulse) she said. '*A leanbh bán!*' (my dear child). Irish often came to her lips like now when she wanted to express her love.

'*A chuisle mo chroí,*' she said, 'I believe what you told me the morning you ran away. I believed it then but I was in too much of a temper to admit it.'

She reached out her hands and I went and knelt by the bed. She put her arms around me, a thing she hadn't done since I was a small child. I was overwhelmed by the sudden-ness of finding myself being embraced by my mother. She held me close and an uncontrollable spasm seized my body and I began to shake. I cried and buried my face in the blankets so that she couldn't see me. Thousands of thoughts milled around in my head. Things I wanted to say to her, but when I raised my head all I could say was, 'I'm sorry!'

I sat on a chair and she told me that she was worried to death while I was away. Expecting every minute that the door would open and I would be standing there. She spoke of my father, who had never uttered a harsh word to me. It was hard on him working alone and trying to cope with all the extra jobs that were coming his way lately.

'Tomorrow,' she said and she was in her old form now, 'he is going building a hayshed for Scanlon.'

She looked at me to see what effect the name would have on me. I thought of Jude as she said it and I suppose I reddened up.

'You are too young,' my mother said, 'to take a thing like that seriously. Your father was twenty-seven before he met me. Take your time, the world is wide. You'll find that Miss Scanlon has other things on her mind. It's only a couple of years since she was going to school. She's too young to take on the cares of life. You wait. She has other plans, you'll see.'

The episode of my running away was at an end and I was happy to be back. I would have dearly loved to talk to my mother as I sat there. To ask her how she met my father and what life was like when she was my age. I wasn't able to bring myself to do it. Somehow some sort of barrier came down when I felt like talking about things like that to her or to my father. We thrashed out the ordinary everyday matters about the house. But when it had anything to do with the heart we were trapped in a web of silence.

'Will you have anything to eat?' she wanted to know.

'I'll have a cup of milk,' I said, 'if it's there.'

'There's plenty of milk,' she assured me, 'and before I forget it. I put them in a paper bag. It's there on the top of the press.'

I looked in the paper bag. It contained Jude's stockings. I put them in my pocket and to cover my embarrassment I went out of the room. 'Good night!' I said to my father as I crossed the kitchen and climbed the stairs to bed.

XVII

Strawboys Come Dancing

The day we went building Scanlon's hayshed was a joyous day for me. I saw Jude going about her household duties, feeding the calves, giving mess to the fowl and drawing water from the well. She drew my mind away from my work and my father had to call on me to pay attention to what I was doing. At about eleven o'clock Jude and her mother brought out two bowls in which there were beaten-up eggs in steaming hot milk with sugar, and a few spoonfuls of whiskey in my father's bowl. It was a drink my father loved; maybe Jude's mother heard somewhere of his liking for it. He thanked the women and told Jude's mother that she had a big heart to go to so much trouble.

'It was no bother at all,' she said. 'You deserve it. Good tradesmen are to be cherished.'

She remarked then that she was related to my mother. Consanguinity again! She and my father began tracing relationships and I was praying that the connection wasn't too near and that it wouldn't be an impediment if Jude and myself ever thought of getting married. 'This boy is your eldest, Ned?' she said to my father, and without waiting for an answer she went on, 'He is a great help to you. Shake

170

hands with him, Jude. Maybe ye know each other already.'

I shook Jude's hand and taking the hint from the gleam in her eye we both acted as if we were meeting for the first time. I was reluctant to look at my father in case he'd spill the beans, but on second thoughts I knew he wouldn't, though my heart missed a beat when he said, 'Nearly all young people know each other now. They get around more than we did, ma'am. The bicycle was a great invention.' Though I was only seventeen I could hardly remember the first time I rode a man's bike; it was so long before. When I started my apprenticeship I got a new model and my father and I cycled everywhere to work.

Dinnertime came and Jude came out to call us. I waited to talk with her until all the men had gone into the house. There was a small moment of embarrassment when I gave her the paper bag with her stockings. Blushing, she concealed the bag under her apron and when we talked about the night of the stepping stones, I never mentioned about my mother finding her stockings in my pocket. We both went into the kitchen. All the places around the large deal table were filled but mine.

'*An té a bhíonn amuigh fuaireann a chuid,*' Jude's mother said (He who is out his portion cools). Old Scanlon sat at the head of the table, a big red-faced man with a sandy moustache and a good cover of thatch on his head. All the talk among the men was about a marriage that was taking place some distance away in a few days' time. Getting married outside Shrove was very rare, but the groom, who had spent some years in the city and was home on early pension from the prison service, had drifted a little from the old customs. It was a made match and he was marrying one of the Galvin girls of the Knob. There was no son in that house and the gaoler was getting the land.

'She's a prisoner now for life,' Old Scanlon laughed.

'And there will be hard labour too,' managed another.

'That'll do,' Jude's mother said, drawing a rein on the conversation before it went too far. 'It will be a great wedding. The Galvins always had the big heart. There'll be no shortage there.'

'What good is that to us,' Old Scanlon replied, 'when we won't be invited? Unless we'd straw. Did you ever straw, Ned?' he asked my father.

Strawboys were the uninvited guests who went to a wedding in disguise for a short visit. They were given a drink and a chance to dance a set, and many groups of them called in the course of a wedding night.

'Many is the time,' my father told him. 'But strawing was an art in the old days. A week would be spent making a straw suit, complete with skirt, cape and high-caul cap. Our faces were blackened or covered with a piece of lace curtain. There was always a captain over a group of strawboys. He was the only one who spoke and the others had to obey him.'

'Surely the girls went strawing as well,' Jude's mother asked. 'We didn't have the custom up our way.'

'Of course they did,' my father replied, 'Where would we be without them!'

'Strawboys in the old days were an orderly enough crowd,' Old Scanlon held. 'They added a bit of variety to a wedding dance. Was our wedding strawed?' he asked Jude's mother.

'By the way he doesn't remember!' she laughed. 'Maybe you were too far gone guzzling Ballyvourney poteen to remember anything.'

'I had a few jorums all right,' Old Scanlon admitted. 'But where's the harm in that. It's only one night in a man's life. My match was a love match, so I had something to celebrate.'

There was talk then of matchmaking. The men said it was

a good system and only for it many would go unmarried. It was a way of bringing people together, especially shy people, and it made sure that the dowry which enabled the groom's sister to marry another farmer was paid. Often the same dowry went the rounds of the parish. Even though those getting married did not know each other until they were brought together some weeks before, they all seemed to get on very well. The men could only think of one case out of all those who had matches made for them which broke down. The young woman returned to her own people the morning after the wedding and if the groom shook gold under feet she wouldn't go back to him. Two lives were ruined for neither could marry again. The fortune she paid was never given back to her, and the men from the two sides belted one another black and blue with ashplants over it every fair day.

In the conversation we heard of a man who was going with a farmer's daughter. They were always together at house dances. The young girl had no brothers and her elder sister, no oil painting, was to get the farm. When Shrovetime came round an account of a match was sent to the elder sister by the young man's parents. The match went ahead and he married the elder sister and lived in the same house with the two women until the young girl went away to America.

'The land he loved and not the woman,' Old Scanlon remarked. 'It was often a man with a big farm and an unpresentable daughter got as fine a man as was going for a son-in-law. The craze for land is great. It is indeed!'

'Men and women,' he continued, 'having spent ten years in America working hard, came back with dowries in their pockets and were in great demand when Shrovetime matches were being made. They settled into new homes with partners they barely knew. With their Yankee clothes and New York accents they were conspicuous for a while, but in a few years, except for the gleam of gold in their teeth, you wouldn't know them from those who never went away.'

Jude had heard all that was said and when I got a chance afterwards I put forward the idea of strawing the wedding on the Knob the following Tuesday night. She was excited about the notion and there and then we decided to get a crowd together to make up a group of strawboys. Six would be enough; three boys and three girls, as many as would make up a set dance. Some evenings before, we came together and with wisps of straw made ropes to put around our lower legs like army puttees. We fashioned bands of straw to place about the waist and shoulders and plaited shorter lengths to decorate out caps. We, the men, turned our coats inside out and the girls, borrowing their fathers' or their brothers' coats did the same thing. With the straw leggings on and our bodies festooned in straw and our faces covered with pieces of old lace curtain, we defied anyone to recognise us. The kick we got out of helping each other to dress and seeing the end effect was tremendous.

We marched together to the house on the Knob, and hung around outside for a while listening to the music and the jollity from within. Then, summing up courage, our captain knocked on the door and chanted:

Strawboys on the threshold,
Strawboys at the door.
Keep a place for strawboys
On the dancing floor.
We wish the bride and groom
The very best of cheer.
May they have a son or daughter
Ere the end of the year!

The bride's father, old Galvin, came forward and made room
for us in the middle of the kitchen floor. The men accepted
a bowl of porter from a large bucket. There was a tint of wine
for the ladies. It was my first time tasting strong drink. I kept
my confirmation pledge until that instant. When the porter
touched my tongue I nearly gasped at the sourness of the
mixture. It was as bitter as the gall which was given to Our
Lord on the cross. The second sup tasted a little better and
I finished the bowl in time with the other men. Then we lined
out for a set dance. The captain spoke to the musicians and
called for a polka set. We tapped the floor in unison, waiting
for the opening note in the music. When it came we started
out around the house. Early in the first figure one couple
danced to the centre while all the others stood by. Guests at
the wedding moved forward and playfully tried to remove
the disguises from our faces. We fought them off and I had
a hard job protecting Jude from the inquisitive advances of
a large man with hands as big as a hayfork. Our costumes
and disguises were much admired as we heeled and toed to
the lively music. There were cheers and much applause at
the antics of some of the dancers. At the end of the last figure
we all wheeled together, our arms encompassing each other
in a tight bunch in the middle of the floor. We swung until
the house and people swung with us and when we came to
a halt our heads were still spinning.

'A song! a song!' the crowd demanded and the captain
called on me to sing 'My Mary of Loughrea'. I held on to the
frame of the room door to steady myself and get my breath
back and then I gave what I considered was a good blast.

The youths will miss you from the dance
On Sunday evenings fair.
The grass will miss your fairy steps

To wash the dews away,
But I will miss you most of all
My Mary of Loughrea!

It was an emigration song and on the last line, which was always spoken, Jude caught and squeezed my hand.

'I have something to say to you tonight,' she said. 'Not now.' I had bent eagerly towards her. 'Later on.'

We said goodbye to the bride and groom and wished them luck. Our captain thanked them for having received us. On our way out there was another group of strawboys. They were admitted and as we crossed the yard a third group arrived. We waited until the second group came out, only to find that the third batch was refused admission. The people of the house, I am sure, thought they had enough of a good thing for one night.

This last bunch proved to be of a very unruly element and cut up rough, shouting, name calling and casting aspersions on the family. They lifted loose stones from the fence and began throwing them on the corrugated iron roof. The din was ear-splitting and drowned out the music. The door opened suddenly and young men from the wedding party rushed out. They waded into the strawboys and there was the father and mother of a fight, lit only by a watery moon. We and the second group made ourselves scarce as we didn't want to be identified with a pack of blackguards. As we legged for home, we could hear those who were refused admission taking to their heels as well. I couldn't help thinking that whichever rogue strawboy met up with the large guest with the hands as big as a hay fork must have come in for a fair hammering.

We got rid of the straw at the next hayshed, turned our coats the right way back and put the lace masks in our pockets. We walked to the oak tree where Jude and I always rested and talked and laughed and courted and kissed. Many were the outlandish things we talked about. I told her about the strange dream I had the night we crossed the stepping stones. There was a silence and a turning away of her head as if she doubted my sanity. We talked of mundane things too like would it rain tomorrow? No. It would be fine. There was no cap of clouds this evening on the twin mountains. The breasts of Dana were clear and plain to be seen. Of course I didn't dare call them that, but I called her Dana, my goddess of the mountain. She laughed, and said I was turning into a prime eejet.

'And don't be associating me with a mountain, two mountains in fact!' she said, pushing me away from her playfully.

We walked the last steps to her father's house. She went inside the small wicket gate and closed it, and with the gate between us she said, 'You remember me mentioning that I had something to say to you tonight?' I waited. The dog barked.

'I won't be seeing you again. I am going to England tomorrow.'

A lump rose in my throat and I couldn't speak. Tonight had been so wonderful. The dressing up, the music, the dance, and Jude and I had been so happy together. The dog barked again. She became uneasy.

'My sister Mary is nursing in England,' she said, 'and I am going over to her. When I am gone, it'll be out of sight out of mind. You'll find someone else.'

I couldn't ever forgive her for saying that. The bottom had fallen out of whatever little world was mine. Her hand was resting on the gate. I placed mine on it and caressed it for a second but no words came and as I turned away she said,

'Goodbye.' I kicked the rambler stones before me on the roadway with temper and disappointment. In anguish I bit my lip and the blood tasted salty on my tongue. The suddenness of her announcement that she was going away really floored me, left me without words. But now phrases and sentences raced through my mind as I realised how bleak my life would be without her. I thought of how she squeezed my hand at the end of the emigration song I sang at the wedding. How sweet that memory was. How sweet was every memory of every moment since the first night I summed up enough courage to ask her to allow me to convey her home from Bryanie's dance.

Even though it was early they were all in bed when I went in home. I went lightly up the stairs but my mother heard me and called me in to my parents' room. She wanted to know how things went at the wedding. She and my father had strawed weddings when they were young. I told her that we were well received and that it was very enjoyable. She was interested in the names of people I saw at it. I thought it better then not to mention about the ferocious fight. Maybe tomorrow.

'I'll be home early every other night,' I told her. 'Jude is going to England.'

My mother must have noticed the sadness in my voice for she said, 'You'll get over it; there are as good fish in the sea as ever were caught. Don't get so involved the next time. It will be many a long day before you settle down. You'll soon forget this canter. Time is the great healer.'

But I would never forget and each disconnected sentence of my mother's echoed in my head as I tried to sleep. I longed for this day to end. To entice the cloak of sleep around me I thought of the first time I laid eyes on Jude, and I recalled each time we met and walked and talked and sang and kissed, our backs to the old oak tree by her father's house. Gradually her face faded and music took over. We were dancing, not at the wedding on the Knob, but on a dancing deck on a Sunday afternoon in Shronaboy. Lough Guitane lake was down below and Lough Léin was in the distance. The mountains were coloured brighter than I had ever seen them. Everything was bright and the light was dazzling. Jude and I were doing the solo piece in the second figure of the dance. It ended in a wheel. The music raced and so did we. I lifted Jude off her feet. She was so light and as we spun the dancers cheered us. There was laughter and loud clapping and then someone shouted, 'the Priest!'

The parish priest drove his car on to the dancing deck, scattering the dancers in all directions. The girls screamed as we barely got out of the way of the Ford car with spurts of steam coming from its radiator. We hid behind the bushes while the fiddler, who was blind, played on. As the priest stepped on to the deck the car began to dance to the fiddler's tune, the wheels in turn lifting off the platform, the horn crazily blowing. Waving his blackthorn stick the priest danced madly, wisps of straw circled his biretta, and he wore a stole of woven straw around his neck. The blackthorn blossomed in his hand and his vestments fluttered wildly in the breeze. We emerged from our hiding place and cheered him on as jets of steam coming from the radiator kept time to the music. Steam soon enveloped the car and the priest's mad, laughing face got lost in the fog. Down below us Lough Guitane lake bubbled and boiled and fish put their heads out of the water and screamed, 'We're scalded!' It must have been the end of the world for the Punch Bowl on Mangerton overflowed its brim and water cascaded down the side of the mountain engulfing us. As we fought our way through the flood I sat bolt upright in the bed, and ended the madness that was churning in my brain.

'You're to be pitied,' my mother said, who had been wakened by my shouting. 'Is there any other boy whose head is so crazed by nightmares? That Jude'll be the death of you!'

XVIII

GOODBYE TO THE HILLS

Concrete was the new building material and the construction of stone houses was becoming rarer as time went on. My father had gained much experience in the use of concrete while building bridges for Singleton after the Civil War, and the making of boat piers in Ballinskelligs and elsewhere. He built the first concrete house in our district. It was for the Galvins on the Knob. The new man, the ex-gaoler, had modern ideas and engaged my father to do the building. I helped to make the casing from the new floorboards to hold the poured concrete. When one layer of cement and gravel mix extending right around the house was set, we undid the bolts, raised and re-bolted the shutters and poured another layer. The house went up as quickly as if four masons were building it in stone. People came and watched the job in progress and the more cynical predicted that the walls wouldn't keep out the damp nor the chimney pull the smoke. In a short time the house stood waiting to be capped with a roof and the dark windows like blind eyes waiting for glass lenses to be put in. When the last stroke had been struck my father went down the field to admire his handi-work. From the laying of the foundation to the turning of the key in the front door he had, with a little help from me, done it all himself. He had been mason, carpenter, joiner, slater, plasterer and glazier.

The family moved in and the cynics were proven half right. The walls were as dry as pepper but the chimney had not as good a draft as a masonry house. The ex-gaoler got over this drawback by installing a turf-burning range, and my father, by studying the work of the old masons, mastered the art of chimney making. In subsequent concrete houses he built, the draft was so great he used to remind the woman of the house with a half-smile to keep the small children back from the fire in case they'd be sucked out the chimney. He was now on his way to becoming, in the eyes of those who begrudged him his success, the concrete king.

We were engaged in the enlargement of an hotel in town, an all-concrete job. One day the proprietor asked me if I intended giving my entire life sawing boards and grouting concrete. I told him that I had every notion of improving myself and that I was taking a correspondence course with the Bennett College in England. He laughed at that. 'Learning carpentry by post!' he said. 'And a fine technical school inside in your own town.'

The building and craftwork teacher at the technical school was the architect of the hotel enlargement project, and the next time he came to the site in his capacity as clerk of works, the proprietor introduced me to him and I said I would like to join his class when it opened at the technical school in September. Meeting this man, Micheál Ó Riada was his name, was the means of changing the direction of my footsteps and putting me on the first mile of a journey that would take me far from my own parish. He taught me and others the craft of wood and in time we passed examinations set by the technical branch of the Department of Education in carpentry, joinery and cabinet making. He taught the theory of building and how to draw and read plans; he taught solid geometry which holds the key to the angles met with in the making of a hip roof or a staircase.

Two nights a week, no matter how far from home my day job was, I cycled to the tech. We, Micheál Ó Riada's students, soon discovered that his interests were not confined to the bench or the drawing board. His passion for music was great, though he didn't like jazz; he thought it a very primitive sound. When his demonstration lesson was over and we were busy sawing and chiselling he put on classical records on an old gramophone in the classroom. Books and writers he talked about, and the theatre.

On the head of this I went one night to see Louis Dalton's company at the Town Hall in *Juno and the Paycock*. It was my first time seeing actors on a stage and the humour, the agony and the tragedy of the play touched me to the quick. I laughed and cried and when I left the hall I walked a mile through the dark, coming to terms with the plight of the Captain's family. O'Casey's characters kept me from sleep that night and I envied the actors their power to draw me away from the real world and almost unhinge my reason long after the curtain had come across. I told Ó Riada about my visit to the town hall. He was interested in my reaction to the play and after class that night he talked to us about O'Casey's other plays. He mentioned the works of J. M. Synge and Lennox Robinson and advised us if ever we were in Dublin to go to the Abbey Theatre.

Ó Riada didn't tell us, but we discovered that he had been interned in Ballykinlar Camp during the trouble. While there he made an illuminated book in Celtic strapwork design in which were the names of all the prisoners. This book is in the War of Independence section of the National Museum.

His interests were even out of this world, and one night when there was an eclipse of the moon he populated the blackboard with planets in their courses, and illustrated how the eclipse came about which was taking place over our heads in the sky. The different timbers he taught us to cherish — from Honduras mahogany to the pale beech of our own woods. The furniture of the fields he called the deciduous parkland trees, and following his illustrations on the blackboard we grew to know these from their outline and the shape of their leaves. We could, after a time, readily recognise the timber that came from them by its colour and the grain of the wood. He could carve, inlay and French polish. He talked to us about nature, and when a class was over and the tools stored away we remained behind discussing with him whatever was the whim of the evening until the caretaker came along jangling his keys. By the time we got our bikes out of the shed he was in the street. He always dressed as if he were heading for some formal occasion. As we put on our bicycle clips we watched him for a moment as he set out in his soft hat and long brown overcoat, carrying a walking stick as he walked with a limp. Before we overtook him and waved 'goodnight' he had passed many shopfronts which he had designed himself. His Celtic strapwork was a feature of fascia boards in our town and as far away as Listowel.

One evening Mr Ó Riada mentioned to me that if I kept making headway in my studies and passed the senior grade in the practical and theory papers he would enter me for a scholarship examination to train as a manual instructor in Dublin. In the meantime, as well as the theory of building and craft work I would have to study English, Irish and maths. I would need a good grounding in these subjects as I had left the national school when I was fourteen. Since then my secondary education had been taken over by the editor of a daily newspaper.

I wasn't long working with my father when the *Irish Press* came out. It was a bright paper with news on the front page instead of advertisements. Newsboys, the first we had seen in town, were on the streets with it on fair and market days. Later during the economic war which raged between Ireland and England and which was brought about by de Valera's withholding of the land annuities, the English put an embargo on our cattle and small farmers had their backs to the wall. Animals were brought to the fair so often that they knew their way in and out of town. In the middle of the Fair Field a newsboy said to a dejected farmer standing by a cow he had failed to sell, 'Press, Sir!'

'Be off,' the farmer replied. 'We have presses at home and nothing in 'em!'

But still the bulk of the people stood behind de Valera in his fight with the British. On his second or third election victory I marched with those same farmers to the village. Each man had a two-pronged hay fork on which was impaled a sod of turf steeped in paraffin oil. At the outskirts of the village the sods were set on fire and we marched down the street in a torchlight procession, stopping and jeering outside the houses of those we knew didn't vote for de Valera. An older man in the company, who had fought against the Tans and the Free Staters, carried a shotgun. Under the light he dismantled the firearm and gave me the stock to conceal inside my coat in case the guards would spot it. But the guards, drawn from a pro-treaty background, kept well out of sight this night. Later on when we had left the barracks behind us, the old IRA man reassembled his gun and discharged both barrels in the direction of the residence of a well-known Cosgraveite. The band played more loudly, smothering the report.

A large bonfire was lit by the ball alley which, with the torchbearers ranged about it, made a memorable scene in the surrounding darkness. There were speeches and tributes to the tall gaunt man with the foreign name who stood against the might of the Empire. Amid the wild cheers and cries of 'Up Dev!' a poor travelling woman, the worse for drink, threw her black shawl on the bonfire. It spread out in the air before landing, then for a moment the fire was blotted out. Soon the flames came through the shawl and a shower of sparks went up. Hannie, for that was the woman's name, pulled out her combs so that her long grey hair fell down over her face, older than the Hag of Beara's. With her arms raised as if in supplication to some strange god she danced around the fire as the Millstreet fife and drum band struck up another tune.

The blood coursed warmly through our veins. There were shouts of 'Up the Republic!' and 'Smash partition!' Stones were thrown into the fire and sent up sparks. The band marched off and Hannie's ancient feet grew weary of the dance. As the music died in the distance the hilarity subsided. Gradually the sods of turf on tops of the pikes burned out and so did the fire. As the light faded from the faces of the crowd anyone who had the price of a pint went with the old IRA man to John Dan's public house. There he demonstrated again, as he had done many times before, the correct way to dislodge a horse policeman, and told how with an old cannon mounted on a railway wagon he and his comrades captured Rathmore RIC barracks. He called for a glass of whiskey for Hannie. The artist deserved her fee. She sang a verse of 'When Sandy Heard the Rifle Fire', but tomorrow without her shawl she would feel the cold, and the small farmers would feel the pinch of the economic war.

Whenever we worked in town or passed through it, I

spent a precious penny on the *Irish Press*. At night I read it from front to back. The sports pages, the book page on Saturdays and the daily contributions of Roddy the Rover which had characters like the garda called Sergeant Gasta MacCliste. There was a section devoted to the Irish language and it galled me that I could not read it as well as I could the English. I was embarrassed by the fact that as a young Irishman my own language was almost a closed book to me. I went back to my old teacher at the national school one night a week to study Irish for the examination. Micheál Ó Riada asked me to come to his house another night to study maths. He gave me some tips on how to write an English composition and helped me with grammar.

All this extra interest outside my work, going to the tech two nights a week, a night studying English and maths and a night at Irish helped to heal the wound caused by parting from my sweetheart Jude. But she remained forever in my mind and in the mornings when I met the postboy I saw him as a link between us. I always expected him to have a letter from her but one never came. I hadn't much time for dancing but I did go to the local house dance on Sunday nights. But the dancers were drifting away. A new dancehall had been built in Barraduv village, a concrete affair with a corrugated iron roof and a boarded floor. The dancers seemed to glory at the effect their dancing feet had on the timber. It sounded like a drum and was a change from the stone-flagged floors of the country kitchens. Visitors from the town introduced old time waltzing. It took some time before I had the courage to venture out in that. When I did we waltzed to the strains of 'Oft in the Stilly Night' and the sound of our feet was quieter than the pounding we gave the floor when out in a set dance. The hall of laughter and music was directly across the road from the church and was the subject of many a sermon by Father Browne.

'The house of God,' he thundered, 'is on one side of the road and the house of Satan at the other!'

A mature spinster from out the Bower claimed as gospel truth that while dancing with a stranger in the house of Satan she looked down and saw a cloven hoof and his hands, she said, were burning hot. The dancehalls were licensed by an Act of the Oireachtas and that notice was prominently displayed above the door. The halls in time sprung up everywhere, putting an end to the house dances which the clergy themselves had been trying to do for years. Many is the time the parish priest and his curate raided the houses where Sunday night dances were held. And even though scouts were posted outside to watch for the beam of the headlights those headlights were turned off at a distance from the house and the raiding party was down on top of the dancers before they knew where they were. One night when the curate stood in the front door the back door wasn't wide enough to take the outflow of dancers into the dung-stained yard in front of the cowhouse. The women, fearful of being recognised by the priest, in an effort to retrieve their coats and shawls from the room got caught in the narrow door. The last lady was so dazed after leaving the light that she ran straight into the parish priest who was coming in the back way. To save himself from falling in the dirty yard and ruining his new top coat he had bought in Hilliard's cheap sale, he put his arms around the young woman and she, struggling to free herself said, 'Bad luck to you! Isn't it hard up you are for your hoult and the priest coming in the front door!'

One young man, our famous full-forward in the football team, remained oblivious to all this. He was courting in a dark corner under the stairs. He never felt a bit until the curate shone the flashlamp on him. He got such a fright it was said that he never scored after!

I never heard of a dancehall being raided by the clergy, but the priest in our neighbouring parish succeeded in persuading the dancehall proprietors in his jurisdiction, as you might say, to close their premises during the hours of darkness. Béalnadeega hall, the nearest one to us until Barraduv Hall was built, opened only on Sunday afternoons. We flocked there and danced until it was time for the farmers' sons and daughters to go home for the evening milking of the cows. As well as the economic war, de Valera had another thorn in his side in the shape of the Blueshirts. These followers of General Eoin O'Duffy arrived in force at Béalnadeega hall one Sunday. They were dressed in their military type shirts and were accompanied by their women, the blue blouses as we called them. Young men of the new IRA and members of Dev's political party resented this intrusion into what they held to be a Republican stronghold. They jostled the blueshirts and the blue blouses while dancing. One provocative shoulder borrowed another, tempers frayed, and while you'd be saying Jack Robinson fists started to fly. The blueshirt women screamed as strong daughters of the Republic tore the blouses off their backs. The blue army retreated, leaving behind the torn shreds of their fascist uniform. Despite what seemed like a murderous onslaught, no blood was spilled and no bones broken. The musicians struck up a dance tune called 'The Cat Rambled to the Child's Saucepan' and with order restored, the dancing continued till the cows came home.

On Monday morning it was back to work for me and that night to my lessons in English and maths at Micheál Ó Riada's house in Rock Road. Wednesday night was given over to the study of Irish and on Tuesday and Thursday nights I went to the tech. I worked hard for the next two years until the time came for me to sit for the scholarship examination. I did my best when the day came and finished the practical test on time. I had to make a joint used on a stairs landing known as a tusk tenon, an intricate affair. Time went by slowly until at last the results came out. I was over the moon. I had got through the test and passed the interview in Dublin as well.

September was now approaching when I would be going from the valley where I grew up. My father was sorry to lose me when I could be of most help to him. But the third son in the family, Laurence, was working at the trade and showing a real talent for the job. The second son, my brother Tim, who was always better than me at school, was in a seminary in Cork and going on to be a missionary priest.

The night before I was due to leave for Dublin I went around to all the neighbours' houses. In each house I sat by the fire and everyone's attention was on me; a kind of curiosity as I was the one going away. We talked about the little incidents, that for us loomed large, incidents that had happened in the district in the twenty odd years of my life. Then it was a hearty shake hands and a good wish for my success. Next morning my mother and father went with me in the pony and trap. I had a new travel bag, a valise my mother called it. The last time my father had driven me to the railway station was when my brother and I were going on the school outing to Rossbeigh. From the platform where we now stood I had seen many young men and women leave for America and I recalled the tearful partings. From here Jude went out of my life. But now as the train from Tralee reversed into the platform I put mournful thoughts aside and got into high spirits, thinking of the new life that lay ahead. No need for fond farewells, my mother said laughingly. I would be home on holidays for Christmas. My father fell silent and, noticing him, I fell silent too as the reversing train blotted out my last look at the tower of the friars' chapel. The guard's green flag was waving as we warmly shook hands. I stood by the carriage window of the moving train until my parents turned to go. I watched them walk slowly away.

We passed under the Countess Bridge where Nelligan's soldiers blew my countymen to bits. Soon we were in the open valley and I could see houses built by my father and myself. I could see houses where I had danced all night and I could see the river Flesk where Jude and I crossed the stepping stones. Things to remember in my old age, and fresh in the mind's eye forever would be that half-ring of hills like a ground row on the stage where my youth was acted out. Nearing Millstreet I put my head out the window and looked westwards towards home. In the distance I could see the twin mountains, An Dá Chích Danann, the Olympus of Ireland. And as the train sped on, the glorious breasts of the goddess Dana gradually sank out of my view.

✗